Patrick Riley lives in Stockport, Cheshire.

SERIOUS DECEIT

Sam Brown and his gynaecology department at the University Hospital of Southern Massachusetts are highly regarded for their standards of work. In contrast, Peter Mendova and his partner, Simone, run their practice to such an illegal extent that they should be facing time in jail. Instead, they are earning hundreds of thousands of dollars . . . Meanwhile, Cindy James, sister in Sam's department, wants to end her marriage to Billy; and young intern Nick Bailey plans to lay as many nurses as he can. None of these individuals realise that their lives are about to intertwine in intrigue, lies and horror.

PATRICK RILEY

SERIOUS DECEIT

Complete and Unabridged

ULVERSCROFT
Leicester

First published in Great Britain in 2005 by
Robert Hale Limited
London

First Large Print Edition
published 2006
by arrangement with
Robert Hale Limited
London

British Library CIP Data

Riley, Patrick
  Serious deceit.—Large print ed.—
  Ulverscroft large print series: general fiction
  1. Hospitals—Massachusetts—Boston—Fiction
  2. Suspense fiction 3. Large type books
  I. Title
  823.9'14 [F]

  ISBN 1–84617–445–7

Published by
F. A. Thorpe (Publishing)
Anstey, Leicestershire

Set by Words & Graphics Ltd.
Anstey, Leicestershire
Printed and bound in Great Britain by
T. J. International Ltd., Padstow, Cornwall

This book is printed on acid-free paper

1

She died right in front of him and there was nothing he could do about it.

Not that he didn't try. He fought tooth and nail, sweated for three hours over her, shouting, demanding, pushing the OR team to their limits, using all the skills and techniques fifteen years of surgery at the sharp end had taught him. But still she died.

He saw it coming, knew it would happen as soon as the anaesthetist said 'pressure's falling again, 80/50.'

She'd bled excessively from the start, but they'd had no choice but to continue. Or lose her anyway. The anaesthetist had kept the blood going in as fast as it had been gushing out until the moment when he said 'pressure's falling' for the second time. Then, in spite of two IVs going full blast, and twelve pints of blood already infused, she began losing it faster than they could put it back — before, they were even halfway through putting things right.

She was only twenty-five. It should have been a happy time for her, finding herself pregnant after eighteen months of marriage to her childhood sweetheart. He had talked to them both when she had been brought into the ER four hours earlier. She had developed abdominal pain that afternoon and, when it became unbearable, had been brought in by her husband. They transferred her to OBGYN where the ectopic pregnancy was confirmed by the scans. He explained to them that the baby had implanted in her fallopian tube instead of her uterus, and that it had grown and grown until it had burst through the small tube and caused internal haemorrhage. There was no choice now, if her life was to be saved, but to operate immediately to remove the bleeding tube and embryo. There might still be a chance of pregnancy later.

Now he was losing her, in spite of his reassurance.

'Are those clotting results back?' he yelled in desperation. 'And what about the fresh frozen plasma?'

'60/30.'

'Give me some more packs.'

The scrub nurse handed them over immediately and he stuffed them down, deep into her pelvis to stem the flow of blood. Within seconds, they had turned scarlet in spite of his efforts.

'40/20 — oh God, V. fib. She's arresting!'

The anaesthetist started banging on her chest, looking at the surgeon for help.

'Get the defib,' he barked, ignoring sterility now, leaving the open abdomen for Nick Bailey, his resident, to put in another pack to try to stem the gush, taking over the CPR.

The anaesthetist returned to his machine, drawing up adrenaline and calcium into his syringes to try to kick-start the heart. The orderly ran to the table with the defibrillator trolley and plugged it in.

'Ready!' he announced.

The surgeon took the electrodes and put them on her chest.

'Clear?' he called.

'Clear,' came the chorus in reply, as they all stood back.

He pressed the button with his thumb and the dying body jumped, as if filled with new energy. They looked at the screen as one, not really needing to, for the monotonous tone of the cardiogram told them the heart was still in asystole — dying.

He turned up the energy and put the electrodes back on her chest again.

'Clear?'

'Clear!'

She jumped, but again the monitor continued its flat, unwavering drone.

'Scalpel!'

Slap! The scrub nurse was good. Very good.

He made a deep incision into the chest, then threw the knife back on to the Mayo tray.

'Rib spreader!'

The scrub nurse put it in place.

He thrust his hand through the incision, finding the heart then squeezing it with his right hand in the final desperate effort of internal cardiac massage.

'Defib.'

She handed him the electrodes and he put them directly on to her young heart.

'Clear!'

'Clear!'

Her body jumped again, the power now coursing directly into the heart muscle to try to bring it back to life.

The monotonous tone came back to haunt them and he put his hand back into the chest to try to pump her blood around her dying body until . . .

Until . . .

Five minutes later he was still squeezing.

'Well?' he asked, knowing the answer.

'Pupils fixed and dilated,' responded the anaesthetist wearily. 'Stop again for a moment.' He ceased his squeezing, grateful for the rest. They exchanged glances as the flat drone resumed, and the anaesthetist gave an almost imperceptible shake of his head, looking down, avoiding eye contact. They all knew it was the end, but they had to wait for him to admit it. It was his case, and everyone knew how hard it was to quit.

He looked at them in turn, but this time he kept his hand by his side, still pumping, but now pumping fresh air as if he couldn't stop trying, yet knowing full well it was over. He looked down at her young face, her mutilated body, then slowly pulled off his mask.

'It's over. Time of death 18.35.'

He continued staring at his patient as if he couldn't accept it, then turned suddenly away from the table.

'Close her up, Nick. Thank you everybody,' he said quietly.

He walked wearily towards the surgeons' room. They watched him go, feeling his anguish. He'd done his best, and they all knew no one could have done better than Sam Brown.

The surgeons' room was where the various specialists — general surgeons, orthopaedists, gynaecologists, urologists — waited for their cases to be anaesthetized and prepared for surgery. Coffee-tables in the centre, chairs around the perimeter walls, a sink and sideboard, a coffee machine and a fridge in one corner and a wall-mounted TV completed the basic arrangements. He threw his theatre cap into the waste bin and slumped into a chair, sitting forwards and staring unseeingly at the floor, his head in his hands. He didn't hear her come in, and looked up with a jump when he felt the touch on his shoulder.

Cindy James, the scrub nurse, kept her hand in place for a moment then withdrew it. She gave a nervous cough, then said, 'We just wanted you to know, Dr Brown, we admired everything you did today. No one could have saved that poor girl . . . ' She gave a small sob, the tragedy becoming clearer to her even as she spoke. 'We . . . we just wanted you to know . . . '

She turned to leave, feeling the tears in her eyes. His voice stopped her for a moment.

'Nurse James . . . Cindy.' He looked up at her. 'All of you worked well today. There was nothing more we could have done. We did our best, and lost her. But thank you. All of you.'

She nodded and left, and he sat back with a large sigh, his head against the back of the chair now, surveying the ceiling, still seeing nothing.

He was a big man, six foot two and muscular. He owed his dark good looks to his French mother and American-Guyanian father. Sam Brown had been an associate professor at the University Hospital of Southern Massachusetts for a year, and had already built up a formidable reputation as an excellent gynaecologist, a good administrator and a successful fund-raiser for his department.

'D-I-C,' he said out loud. *Diffuse intravascular coagulation.* When the bleeding body consumes and exhausts its own clotting factor until there is none left, and the bleeding becomes uncontrollable, persistent, fatal.

He had seen it before a few times. Unpredictable, irrational, occasionally controlled by infusion of fresh frozen plasma and other clotting substitutes, but often progressive and deadly.

A vision of her young husband flashed across his mind, and he shook his head slowly. He would be sitting in the waiting area now, occasionally standing to pace the room, glancing at his watch, looking at the door, longing for it to open to reveal a smiling nurse coming to tell him everything was OK, not knowing it would be Sam Brown who was about to open that door, unsmiling, serious, asking him to sit, watching realization dawn on him that something was wrong. Perhaps something minor, she's lost a little blood . . . or something more serious, *it was worse than we thought — we had to remove the uterus . . . she'll never have children . . .* but never expecting what he might really say.

And so it went.

'I'm sorry, Mr Brookes. There were problems, she bled a lot, uncontrollably, then her heart stopped. We did everything we could to revive her but . . . our efforts were in vain. Mr Brookes, your wife is dead. I'm sorry.'

The young man's attentive look was slowly replaced by a frown, as Sam's words sank in. He gave a small shake of his head, as if not believing what he was hearing, and looked down at his hands, which were clasped together so tightly that the knuckles were a tense, bloodless white. Then he looked up at him again.

'Dead?'

It was only a hoarse whisper which came from his dry lips, but for Sam the sound was deafening. The young man cleared his throat, and croaked, 'Dead?'

Sam nodded. 'I'm sorry.' He knew the words would mean nothing.

The young man stood up and turned his back, walking towards the door, as if expecting to see his wife on the other side.

'Dead? Shirley's dead?' The words were louder now as confusion gave way to anger. He turned to face Sam.

'How? Why? Shirley's *dead*?'

He looked directly into Sam's eyes, seeing his unwavering look, seeing the slow nod of the head, realization sinking in that the love of his life had been taken from him. Forever.

Sam knew he would crumple at that point, and he did. It was like his legs suddenly became fluid, unable to support his body, and Sam moved forward quickly to stop him falling, holding him up, guiding him to a chair, supporting him.

After all, he had just let his wife die.

*   *   *

It was late when he left the hospital. The Boston sky was already dark and cloudy and the first hint of winter was in the October air. He pulled up his coat collar as he walked down the front steps towards the staff parking-lot. He reached the car, pressed the alarm button on his keys and opened the driver's door, throwing his briefcase on to the passenger seat. He got in and shut the door, putting the key into the ignition and hearing the confident subdued roar of the Porsche 904 engine come to life accompanied by the soundtrack of *Les Mis* on the stereo: ' . . . singing the songs of angry men . . . '.

Normally he would have cruised out of the lot to his home in Cambridge. Instead, he slowly laid his head forward on to the wheel and sat motionless, listening to the tape until the music stopped. Eventually, he gave a long sigh, sat back, rubbed his eyes, and slid the shift to drive, and the car slowly exited the hospital parking-lot to take an exhausted and demoralized Sam Brown home.

Cindy James watched him walk to his car. She knew what he was feeling and wanted to go to him, but she knew it couldn't be. She admired Dr Brown, and loved working with him in gynaecology; sometimes the urge to tell him that was almost overwhelming, but she never even came close. Until tonight, when she just had to say something on behalf of the whole team to lessen the burden it was obvious to everyone he was carrying. She waited at the top of the steps until he got into his car then began walking down, pausing when the car didn't move. She moved on slowly, only quickening her pace when eventually she saw the Porsche glide out of the parking-lot. She reached her own car and got in, wondering what might be waiting for her when she got home.

* * *

Billy James sat slumped in the chair, the bourbon bottle cradled in his lap as he tried to focus on the talk show on TV. Jerry Springer was getting the worst out of a sad trio from Tennessee involved in incest and wife beating. Through the blur, Billy was cheering on the skinny-ribbed husband and yelling insults at his obese wife. He turned his head when he heard the apartment door open.

'That you?' he yelled.

There was no answer. He shrugged and returned to the bourbon and the TV.

Cindy James walked through the living-room to the kitchen, barely giving her husband a glance. She placed the supermarket bags on the sideboard and started to unpack them.

'What's for dinner?'

She ignored the enquiry and continued her task, remembering the case that afternoon.

The blow took her by surprise. She felt the fist hit her behind her right ear and felt herself falling, scattering the groceries every-where, thinking irrationally that she must tidy them up later.

'Don't you ignore me, bitch! When I ask

something, you answer, you hear?'

She felt the kick on her thigh and groaned, before grabbing the sideboard and hauling herself to her feet.

He was standing in front of her, his left hand clutching the half-empty bourbon bottle, his right hand closed in a fist.

'You're drunk again,' she said, realizing the futility of the statement even as she uttered it.

'Yeah, and you're late. Where the fuck you been? Playing around with your fancy surgeons again? Instead of getting your ass home to make my dinner?'

He aimed another drunken kick at her, but she saw it coming and avoided it, at the same time turning to open a drawer in the kitchen unit.

He staggered towards her, pausing when he saw the knife.

'Billy James, you back off. Back off now or I'll use this; I swear, I'll use it . . . ' She waved the knife towards him to leave him in no doubt of her intent, and he jumped back, almost falling. He tried to focus on the knife, on her, then again on the knife, before shrugging and turning towards the living-room again, banging into the wall as he tried to negotiate the door, swearing to himself.

She watched him go, shaking slightly, even though this was not the first time the scene had been enacted. She opened the drawer and replaced the knife, looking behind her to make sure he had really left. She shut the drawer, turned and leaned against the sink, shutting her eyes for a moment, wondering why she stayed with this man. Even though she knew the answer: 'For better, for worse.' Cindy O'Riordan, second generation Irish. A Catholic background . . . A Catholic wedding . . . 'Till death do us part.'

Inseparable. At least by the spiritual rules she had grown up with, the rules which had governed her infancy, her childhood and her marriage. Until now.

She recalled the feel of his shoulder when she had touched Sam Brown. She had been almost unable to take her hand away. And, when he had turned his head, and said, 'Nurse James . . . Cindy . . . '

Cindy. If he only knew what she was really like, her home, her husband, her miserable life. A tear pricked her eye when she thought of what might have been, and what was reality.

She heard the belch from the next room, and then the loud snore, and sighed, not for the first time in her marriage wondering what she must do to free herself from her captivity.

2

1171 Revere Street, a tall building on the edge of Copley Square in the heart of downtown Boston, is leased mainly by attorneys, accountants, business corporations, and doctors. The plate outside Suite 23A noted the occupant to be a Dr Peter Mendova, MD, Obstetrician and Gynae-cologist. Adverts in the papers referred to Dr Mendova as being *a specialist in human fertility and assisted conception*, with diplo-mas and degrees from major hospitals on the Eastern seaboard, as evidenced also by the framed certificates and testimonials on the walls of the sumptuously furnished offices within suite 23A.

They were all fakes.

Dr Peter Mendova was a graduate MD who had barely scraped through medical school, whose only ambition in life was to use his medical degree to make as much money as possible as quickly as possible. For this purpose, he needed a post on a residency programme. He had always favoured gynae-cology. He liked women. Liked looking at them, talking to them, examining them, often lingering, appearing to be professional and thorough while he savoured the moment.

And it was clear that they liked him too, the good-looking young student in the white coat.

So that part was easy. As for the rest of it, surgery, general medicine, care of the elderly, pathology, they were all so boring to him that he was amazed he managed to get through his finals.

Yet graduate he did, to begin his pursuit of a career in OBGYN — obstetrics and gynaecology. But his attempts to get on a residency programme were never successful and, after many failed interviews, he seemed destined for a tedious career as a general practitioner, until that night in New York.

After another unsuccessful interview at Cornell, he was sitting at a downtown Manhattan bar, drinking himself into oblivion, when she came up and sat beside him. There were several empty stools, but she ignored them and sat down right beside him. He looked up at her fleetingly. About twenty-seven, trim figure, blue eyes, short blonde hair, tanned features. She looked vaguely familiar but he couldn't place from where. He returned to his glass, wondering why she had chosen to sit next to him. A hooker? A naive tourist? Or just a confident New-Yorker waiting for her boyfriend?

'Hi!'

The word took him by surprise and he almost spilled the beer heading for his mouth. He took a gulp and looked at her.

'Hi,' he responded, before returning to his Budweiser.

'You waiting for someone?'

She certainly was sure of herself.

'No,' he replied.

'I'm Simone, Simone Belmont.' She turned towards him, holding out her hand. He took it in his, and felt it hold on after he thought the handshake was over.

'Peter Mendova,' he responded. 'Can I buy you a drink?'

'Thanks. Whisky-dry. Johnnie Walker. I saw you at the interviews this afternoon,' she said.

So that was why she looked familiar. He remembered now, he had passed her in the corridor leading to the interview-room as she came out and he went in.

'I didn't get the job either,' she continued.

'Trying for an OBGYN residency too?'

'Yep. Some hope. The guys applying are far ahead of me. My CV just isn't in their league.' She shrugged. 'I may have to reconsider.'

He nodded glumly. 'Me, too. I like the subject though. And there's big bucks to be got out there.'

'Sure is. Big bucks. Don't think I've not thought about it.' She looked him directly in the eye as she said it.

He felt vaguely uncomfortable, but he ordered more drinks and they made small talk as she glanced at him, sizing him up. He knew she would approve. Twenty-eight, dark, almost Spanish complexion, big brown eyes, muscular build. He never had a problem attracting women.

After a few minutes he finished his beer and put the glass down purposefully on the bar.

'Look, Simone, I don't know you and I don't know about you, but I'm in a bad mood; I'm really pissed off with today. Another fucking job I didn't get. I'm going to find a few bars, a club maybe, and get tanked up. I'm staying over in a hotel downtown so I've no plane to catch.' He paused. Then said, 'Want to join me?'

He waited for her to say no — *got to get back to the boyfriend, the fiancé, the job.*

Instead she turned to him and said, 'Those are exactly my plans, Peter, so why don't we do it together?'

Thus is was that they moved on to O'Reilly's Bar, to Rosie O'Grady's, then to Tads for a steak, and finally to The Deck for some serious dancing and hard drinking with a little speed thrown in for good measure. Eventually, at around 4 a.m. they staggered back to her hotel as if they had been together for years, laughing and giggling as they waited for the elevator. He saw her to her room.

'Well, thanks for a great evening,' he slurred, as she rummaged for her key. She found it at last and opened the door.

'Not yet, Peter,' she said, taking his hand and almost dragging him into the room. She shut the door behind them turning immediately and pulling him to her, finding his lips, her tongue working on his until she felt him rising against her.

'Come with me,' she whispered, leading him to the bedroom where she began stripping him, his tie, his shirt, then his shoes, his trousers and shorts, before he unzipped her skimpy cotton dress and slipped off her panties. He moved her backwards on to the bed and fell on to her. They made love all night, time and time again, until they fell into an exhausted sleep as the dawn crept into the room through the crack between the curtains.

In the months that followed, Peter Mendova and Simone Belmont fell into deep and passionate love. Within those months they also embarked on a course of events so outrageous, so immoral, and so lucrative, that Peter Mendova more than once thanked his lucky stars for that night in New York when she walked into his life, for he realized that, together, they were going to make all his wildest dreams come true.

* * *

Sam Brown rarely went to funerals of his patients, mainly because not many patients in obstetrics and gynaecology died. It was a pretty rare event. But even when they did, the surgeon's part in the life history of the individual was already over. Unless he was sued, in which case the involvement would drag on for months, years even, until the lawyers were sufficiently fat from the pickings of the case that they settled and moved on to the next piece of litigation.

Shirley Brookes' case was different. This young woman's death, and the plight of her husband, had shaken Sam to the core of his professional soul. He had his secretary make enquiries after the inquest and, on identifying the location of the funeral, slipped into the little church on Manchester Street after the entourage of relatives and mourners had entered. He sat in a corner pew at the back to watch the service. Just as he had settled, a young woman in a raincoat and headscarf walked in, and looked around for a place to

19

sit. She caught Sam's eye and he recognized her immediately.

'Cindy — over here,' he whispered, beckoning her.

Her eyes widened with surprise for a moment before she walked over and sat down beside him. They watched the service in silence and sadness. As it concluded, and the pall bearers made to collect the coffin for the procession to the burial place, Sam whispered, 'We should leave now.'

'If you like,' she replied, 'but we don't need to slip away and hide; we have nothing to be ashamed of here, Dr Brown. We did nothing wrong. We're paying our respects, just like the family. It's only right.'

He paused, looking at her, weighing up her words. Eventually he responded. 'We'll wait.'

He wondered what the family's reaction would be when they saw him. The inquest had been a bitter affair, as they always were, the family seeking some sort of explanation, someone to blame, while the medical examiner attempted to see justice done, if only by making it clear to the family that everything possible had been done and there was no blame. If there was blame, the medical examiner would always say so.

On this occasion, he had not. *Death by Natural Causes.*

The organ music accompanied the passage of the coffin. The family walked past them without a glance, consumed by their own grief.

Sam and Cindy waited a few minutes in the silence of the now empty church before leaving. The cortege was winding its way towards the cemetery. After watching for a few moments, Sam said, 'I think I'll call it a day now.'

'Me, too,' replied Cindy.

Sam nodded. He looked at his watch. It showed 3.30 p.m.

'Can I buy you a coffee or something?'

'You don't need to do that,' she replied nervously.

'I know I don't need to, but I'd like to. I could use company right now.'

'Well, OK. Anywhere you can suggest?'

'There was a little bistro just along the road before the turn to the church.'

She remembered it. They walked to the parking-lot and left in their own cars. Five minutes later, they were sitting in a booth in the bistro drinking latte.

'Do you do this often?' Sam asked, with a wry grin on his face.

'What?' she asked. 'Go to patients' funerals, or have coffee with the surgeons?'

He laughed. 'Both, or neither.'

She laughed too. 'I was surprised to see you here, Dr Brown. Nurses occasionally do go to funerals if the patient was somehow special to them — a case like this, or someone you've nursed personally for a long time. But I've never known a doctor do it.'

He looked into his coffee. 'A first for me. But, like you said, this one was special. And please, call me Sam.'

She nodded, wondering how she could. He was always *Doctor Brown* to the OR staff.

'You were very good that day, Cindy, very good indeed. How long have you worked at UHSM?'

'A couple of years all told, but only three months in the OBGYN OR.' She felt flattered at his comments. Even though she prided herself that she was good at her work, it was always nice to hear it from someone else, especially someone of Sam Brown's professional standing.

He cleared his throat. 'Can I ask you something personal?'

'Of course.'

After a moment he asked, 'Are you married?'

She paused, wanting with all her heart to say say *no* . . . Finally, she gave in.

'Yes . . . why?'

He fidgeted in his seat. 'I just needed to know. I was, uh, going to ask you out for dinner or something but . . . I'm sorry to have presumed.' He looked around as if to find the waitress, embarrassed at his question.

Cindy took a breath then said quietly but firmly, 'Doctor Brown, I'm married to a no-good, lazy, alcoholic ex-cop who I am in the process of leaving. If you were to ask me out to dinner, I would gladly accept. In fact, nothing would give me greater pleasure than to have a civilized dinner with a civilized man in a civilized restaurant. But if you were thinking of repeating that invitation, you'd have to know that, legally, and in the eyes of everyone else who knows me, I'm married.'

She held his gaze without flinching. He was working it out.

'I see,' he said eventually.

She realized he was regretting ever getting into the situation, and wanted out. She did it for him.

She gathered her purse, smiled at him and said, 'Thanks for even thinking of it Dr Brown . . . Sam. I appreciate it, and I've really enjoyed being with you like this.'

He got up from the table with her, and they walked to the pay desk.

'On me, please,' he said, handing over a twenty-dollar bill.

They walked to the door. As he stood back to let her through, he noticed the bruise over her right mastoid bone behind the ear, which she had tried to cover with make-up and her hair, and the scarf she had not yet put back on. They paused on the sidewalk.

'Well, see you at the hospital,' she said.

'Sure thing.'

She turned to leave, filled with contrasting emotions, pleasure at the afternoon, disappointment that she hadn't lied about being married, and that he had not asked her again. But she knew it was hopeless. He'd have found out sooner or later, and why should he get involved with someone like her anyway?

She got into her car and left without looking back.

It was after ten when the phone rang. Billy was out at some sports bar with his cronies. She was at the dining-room table, going over her accounts, wondering just how to start the process of filing for divorce on the grounds of cruelty. She picked up the receiver.

'Yes?'

'Is that Mrs James?'

'Yes. Who is this?'

She knew already.

'Cindy, it's me, Sam Brown. If this is not convenient, just say.'

'It's OK, I'm alone.'

'I won't keep you. I only want your straight answer.' There was a pause, then, 'Will you

24

have that civilized dinner with me one evening next week? No hidden agendas, just dinner?'

'Yes, Sam,' she said without hesitation, 'I will.'

'Thanks. I'll speak with you later.'

The phone went dead. She sat staring at it for a few moments before returning to her work, more than ever determined to change her life, once and for all.

3

Nick Bailey was in a good mood. A very good mood. He had been Fellow in OBGYN at the University Hospital of Southern Massachusetts for just two weeks but already he knew he had made the right choice when he decided to come to Boston. Life was good at home in Melbourne, but he had always wanted to do part of his training abroad. He had seriously considered the UK. Two of his best pals doing urology had jobs there with the big names — George, Kirby, Fitzpatrick, giants in the world of urology — and encouraged him to join them. But Nick wanted something different, and when the exchange fellowship in Boston came up, he jumped at the chance. And he knew it was the right move. The department was world famous and his new boss, Sam Brown, seemed to be a fantastic guy to work with. Socially it was a bit too soon to say, but hell — Boston, major university hospital, good-looking, fit young doctor with a great Aussie accent and all those fantastic-looking young nurses and health-care assistants he'd already clocked — well, there shouldn't be a problem there! He had just listened to the commentary of the semi-final of the Rugby World Cup and, as if to emphasize this period of wonderful good fortune for him, his beloved Australia had eased into the World Cup final to meet their old enemy — England.

Oz v The Poms. Perfect.

He would have had a few beers to mark the achievement except it was his first night on call. Shame, a few tinnies of Fosters, or Buds more likely in Boston, would have gone down well. Buds — he would have to get used to that! Yes, things were looking good as he climbed into bed.

They weren't looking quite as good at 3 a.m. when he was called from the delivery suite. 'Obstructed labour with foetal distress, Doctor — we need help down here now!'

He pulled on his OR greens and cleaned his teeth at the same time before running from his room in the direction of the OBGYN delivery wards. A nurse was waiting at the door. 'In here, Doctor.'

The patient was lying on her back in lithotomy position, her legs up in slings.

'What have you got?'

Chris Hardy, the practitioner nurse, stood up to face him.

'Thirty-three year old, first child, long labour, patient exhausted, deep transverse

27

arrest,' she said. 'Can't reverse the lie with the Keillands forceps. She needs a C-section.'

'I agree. Let's get to it. Epidural OK?' He glanced at the anaesthetist as he moved to the scrub area.

'Epidural fine and she's sedated. No problem.'

No problem. Nick had done many sections before and felt no qualms at the prospect. No previous pregnancies or C-sections, deep transverse position, should be a quick smash and grab. He got to the table and took the scalpel off the nurse, making a low deep transverse incision through the skin and muscle above the pubis to reach the uterus.

Mmm, he thought, this tissue seems unusually thick. But hell, we've got to open the uterus and get this little baby out. He could feel the foetus now and completed the incision to reveal the head. He pushed his hands in and pulled out the child with a feeling of triumph, handing him over to the nurse. He heard the practitioner nurse assisting him speaking.

'Excuse me, Doctor, but what's this?'

He looked down to where Chris was indicating, seeing a light-blue silicone tube lying in the depths of the wound.

'Shit, it's the urinary catheter. We must have damaged the bladder.'

He gently manipulated the tissues as, slowly but surely, realization dawned on him that *damage* was perhaps an understatement. It became clear over the next few minutes that this girl's pelvis was full of inflammatory endometriosis, and that this had stuck the bladder to the front of the uterus until they were firmly attached. As the uterus had expanded slowly with the pregnancy, it had pulled up the bladder with it, so the thick tissue he had noted on the way in was in fact the bladder, completely out of its normal position, plastered on to the front of the uterus. And to get to the baby, he had gone right through the front wall, then the back wall of the bladder. He felt the perspiration break out over his entire body.

'My God,' he gasped, 'what have I done?'

The bladder was lying in two halves in the depths of the wound.

He left the table, looking for the telephone.

'Over there in the prep room, Doctor,' said the nurse, sensing his plight.

'Doctor Brown, Gynaecology, please,' he said, then put the phone down. Within a minute it rang, making him jump.

He explained what had happened to his boss, then put the phone down.

'He's coming in. He's calling the duty urologist also. He said to wait for him.'

'No sweat,' said the anaesthetist. 'She's stable.'

Nick rescrubbed and went back to the table.

'Swab please.' He took the swab from the nurse and put it on to the bottom half of the bladder to soak up any urine that might pass until his boss came, which he did about fifteen minutes later. He scrubbed and came to the table to examine the situation. Nick started to speak but Sam raised his hand to stop him, making him feel even more worried and vulnerable.

After a couple of minutes Sam spoke. 'This is the worst case of endometriosis I've seen for some time,' he said slowly. 'There is no way you could have dissected the bladder off the pregnant uterus to get the baby out, and while the uterus was distended, there was probably no way you could have recognized the tissue as bladder anyway.' He looked up at the young Australian doctor.

'It wasn't anyone's fault, Dr Bailey. You did the right thing and saved the baby. Now the uterus is decompressed, we can see the situation much more clearly. Why don't you repair the uterine incision while we wait for Dr Sinclair to arrive.'

Nick's hands were shaking from the whole experience, and from the relief at the words he had just heard, but he took the needle holder and suture off Chris Hardy, who gave him a small wink of encouragement as he began to repair the wound. As he completed it, James Sinclair arrived and scrubbed as Sam Brown told him what had happened.

'Crikey!' His English accent sounded slightly strange in the Boston operating-room but they had all got used to it since his arrival the previous year.

'Never seen anything like this before,' he continued, rekindling Nick's discomfiture. He looked up at the young Australian, realizing his situation.

'Sorry, Doctor, I'm not trying to blame you; it's just that I've never seen the results of delivering a baby through the bladder before. The good news is that your incisions produced a very clean cut and it should be repairable. Just got to make sure that the ureters weren't damaged. That might raise a problem.'

He passed a fine flexible ureteric catheter through each hole where the ureters from the kidneys enter the bladder and breathed a sigh of relief as they passed easily up to the kidney.

'I'll leave these in place while I repair the bladder to protect the ureters. You can see that on the left here the cut only just missed it, so we must be careful not to snag it up in one of the sutures. That might lead to obstruction later.'

Nick nodded.

'You assist him, Nick,' said Sam. 'See the case through. I'll grab a coffee.'

Sam pulled off his mask and left the OR. They joined him an hour later.

'All done,' said James. 'She should be fine in a few days. We'll have to leave the catheter in for a week though, till everything heals and becomes watertight. I'll look in on her daily.'

'I don't know what to say,' said Nick. 'Nothing like this has ever happened to me before.'

Sam smiled. 'There's always a first time. It was unavoidable, but the main thing is you've seen it and you'll learn from it. That's the secret of surgery — experience.'

The sun was rising when Nick once more climbed into bed, mentally and physically shattered, and almost wishing he had not come to Boston after all.

★ ★ ★

'So, Mr and Mrs Davidson — may I call you Keith and Elizabeth? — it's results and decision time.'

Peter Mendova was sitting in his office in Copley Square. On the other side of the large teak desk sat a couple in their early thirties. Both were smartly dressed; Keith Davidson with dark hair slicked back with mousse, was wearing a dark business suit, smart shirt, bright tie consistent with his job as a computer software representative for a large multi-national company. His blonde wife Elizabeth was equally smart in a beige two-piece suit with matching shoes, and a bright cerise blouse.

Boston high flyers. High achievers, but for one thing — they were having trouble making the family they had decided was to be the next Davidson corporate objective.

'Well, Doctor, we're waiting.' Keith sounded nervous.

'I'll come straight to the point, Keith. My tests confirm those of your previous specialists. Your semen analysis is poor, very poor.' Mendova put on his half rims and looked at the sheet of paper on the desk. 'I'll read them to you, and compare them with normal. Volume: one millilitre; normal four to six millilitres; count: an occasional non-motile sperm; normal, greater than sixty million per millilitre; motility: too few to assess.'

He looked up at the couple. Keith looked angry, his wife had a resigned look on her face. She'd heard it all before, at the Brigham, at Einstein, at the office of the urogynaecologist she had been seeing.

'Your clinical examination revealed testicles at the lower limit of normal size; your pituitary gonadotrophins — ' He broke off for a moment to look at them. 'That's a mouthful, isn't it?' he said, with a smile.

Keith's response was a shrug; Elizabeth looked at the doctor as if she could easily slip a knife into his heart — *I know what pituitary gonadotrophins are, you jerk! You don't get this far down the infertility road without learning that.*

'What it means,' Mendova continued, working to a frequently practised script, 'is that your testicles are not making sperms. Your pituitary gland' — he indicated his head to demonstrate where that would be — 'is driving the testicles to work better by increasing the levels of the circulating hormones, but the testicles are doing the best they can already and are not responding.' He looked up at the couple, slowly removing his spectacles. 'It's a hopeless case, I'm afraid.'

'Hopeless?' Keith almost shouted the word. 'The last doctor we saw told us that he might be able to take a sperm direct from my testicle and inject it into one of Elizabeth's eggs under a microscope. What was that called, Lizzie?'

'ICSI,' she sighed. 'Intracytoplasmic sperm injection.'

'I see,' said Mendova slowly, 'and how much was he going to charge you for that?'

'Twenty thousand dollars.'

There was silence for a few moments until Mendova spoke.

'I won't make any unethical comments, Mr Davidson, but to believe that anyone could puncture your testicle blindly with a needle, and come up with even one suitable sperm, with your sperm count, is to believe in fairy-tales. Expensive fairy-tales.'

'I knew it, Dr Mendova,' Elizabeth Davidson said, flashing a look of triumph at her husband. 'That's why we're here for what seems like our tenth second opinion. I want someone to give us the bottom line so that we can get on with our lives.'

'The bottom line, as I see it, is this: we all have to face the fact that Keith is not going to father a child of his own.' He watched as his patient's shoulders sagged slightly. 'Therefore, the only options available are artificial insemination with donor semen, AI or AID; I prefer to call it AI for obvious reasons, or adoption.'

'As I thought,' Elizabeth said quietly.

'I think you both need to talk this through.'

'We already have,' replied Elizabeth. 'I've

suspected this for some time. Keith's not keen on either, because neither of these options gives us his baby. I am more enthusiastic. Just because it can't be Keith's, why should I be deprived of the chance to have this life-experience? And it would be ours, Keith, from the moment of conception.' She squeezed her husband's hand, and he gave just the hint of a reluctant nod.

'Are you absolutely sure about the sperm counts, Doctor?' he asked.

Mendova leaned back in his chair. 'How many semen samples have you given in the past three years, sir?'

Davidson shrugged. 'It seems like a thousand.'

'And have any of them given you or your doctors encouragement?'

'They've varied from an occasional sperm to none at all.'

'An occasional *immature* sperm, no doubt, incapable of fertilization.'

There was silence for a moment before Elizabeth Davidson spoke.

'How safe is your donor sperm, Doctor?'

'Totally safe. It's collected exclusively from volunteer Harvard students, all of whom are screened for HIV, hepatitis, and any other abnormalities. Any samples with greater than ten per cent abnormal forms are discarded.

The samples are kept in the deep freeze, all labelled for identification. However, that identification is known only to me and my associate, and is never revealed to the recipients. It's a legal requirement. The semen donor signs away any rights to the sample, and its potential progeny. We always attempt to match the donor characteristics to those of the adoptive father.'

'And the success rate?'

'Forty per cent, with a slight predominance of male babies.'

The couple exchanged glances. Almost excited by the prospect.

'Six attempts, like other places?'

'As many attempts as you can tolerate or afford, Mrs Davidson. The charge is two thousand five hundred dollars per attempt, with a further payment of two thousand five hundred if . . . I should say *when* . . . successful.'

They nodded. He knew they could afford it. He paused for a moment before continuing. He was about to make them an offer they certainly were not expecting.

'As an alternative, or if this treatment is unsuccessful, it is possible that I may shortly have access to a small supply of young, very young, babies of both sexes.'

The Davidsons looked at each other, then

back at the doctor.

'Oh?' Keith Davidson sounded sceptical, defensive. 'How is that possible?' he asked. 'I thought the adoption agencies were always bereft of babies? Do you mean Romanian babies or something?'

'No. These will be all-American babies. I have made an arrangement with a religious charity that takes care of unwanted teen pregnancies where, for one reason or another, abortion is not an option. You know, religious beliefs and the like. You would be surprised how many teen pregnancies are occurring these days. In many cases, the natural mother doesn't want to, or can't, keep the baby, and the family wishes to keep the whole thing quiet. The charity is just grateful to me that I might be able to act as an intermediary and place the babies in good homes.'

'And how much will that cost?'

'That will be more expensive, I'm afraid, probably in the region of fifty thousand dollars.'

Keith Davidson whistled.

'I know. It seems a lot. But consider what you have paid already for your 'ten second opinions', along with all the tests. Ten thousand?'

'Nearer fifteen.'

'And say, just say, you have a minimum of

six AIs. That's another fifteen thousand. You're up to thirty now, possibly forty if you keep trying longer. The fifty thousand guarantees you a live, healthy infant *now*.'

The couple exchanged glances again.

'Is it legal?' asked Keith.

Mendova sat back in his chair with a pained look on his face. 'Mr Davidson, what do you take me for?'

'I . . . I'm sorry,' he replied. 'I had to ask.'

'Look around this office, sir. I am one of the best qualified gynaecologists in this city, indeed this state. And one of the best in terms of results. Do you think I would jeopardize any of this by doing something illegal?'

'I guess not. It's just that I haven't heard much about this adoption thing.'

'Nor would you. Given the sensitive nature of the young mothers, and their families, and the requirements of the religious charity, this arrangement is not advertised and is not promoted. Indeed, we ask our clients and patients to be discreet also in these matters. You would not meet, nor know the identity of the mother, but you can be quite comfortable that all your legal rights would be guarded by a formal adoption process.'

Elizabeth Davidson spoke next. 'Doctor Mendova, I want to thank you from the bottom of my heart. After these past two years of struggling and testing, hoping and despairing, you are the first person who has given us hope, real hope, of having a family of our own.' She looked at her husband. 'Keith?'

'Yes, I think you're probably right, Lizzie. But we need to talk it through — which option, combine the two, work out the costs — you know?' He turned to Dr Mendova. 'Can we see you next week with a decision, Doctor?'

'Of course. No problem. Same time, same place?'

'That would be fine.'

They stood up and shook hands, Keith with a serious look on his face, his wife giving Mendova a warm smile.

As they walked towards the door, Keith Davidson paused and turning back, said, 'Doc, I'm sorry for what I said about — '

Mendova cut in. 'That's OK, Keith. It was perfectly reasonable. Sorry if I seemed angry about it.'

'No, not at all. Goodbye, Doctor.'

They closed the door behind them, leaving Mendova alone. He sat down at the desk with a small smile on his face.

They would be back. Probably for a combination of three — four AIs, and adoption if that was unsuccessful. He recalled her smile. It was always the same, almost as if she was entering into a liaison with him, knowing that he would be the one who would give her the child. Which of course he would be. Either way.

But not as they imagined.

4

They met in the lobby of the Ritz Carlton and walked to Sam's car. He drove down towards the Cape, leaving 193 at Junction 12 and heading towards Snug Harbour and the Surf 'n' Turf Restaurant. At first the talk was just pleasantries, but soon they became comfortable with each other and, by the time they had finished their cocktails, it felt to Cindy like she had known Sam Brown a long time. She was a good-looking girl, not beautiful in the accepted or even the contemporary sense of the word, but she had a firm, full figure, tanned complexion, shoulder-length light-brown hair worn in a French pleat this evening, and piercing green eyes in an attractive, honest face.

'This is lovely, Sam. Have you been here before?'

'No, one of the guys at work recommended it. I thought we ought to go out of town . . . '

'Sure. It's better.'

The waiter took the order. He chose grilled swordfish with brown rice and tomato salad, while Cindy ordered jerk chicken with long grain rice and green salad.

'Wine?' he asked.

'Sure. You choose.'

'White or red?'

'Should be white I suppose?'

He sensed the tone of her voice. 'I prefer red too.' He laughed, and they settled for Sutter Home Merlot.

He sat back and sipped the cocktail, looking at her.

'You OK?' he asked, a loaded question if ever he had asked one.

'Yes. I'm entirely comfortable. What about you?'

He gave a small shrug. 'I guess I feel a little uneasy having dinner with a married woman from my own hospital. The thing is, I don't feel I'm doing anything wrong, hurting anybody. Most people wouldn't see it that way, but . . . ' He gave the same shrug again.

'Do you date much?' she asked. 'You're not married, are you?'

She suddenly took a deep sigh and put her hands to her mouth. 'Sorry! Two nosy questions at once!'

'It's no and no,' he smiled. 'I never met the right person to marry, and I've only dated a couple of times since I got here. You're the first girl I've taken out alone on a one-to-one for dinner. Where are you from, Cindy?'

'My father was a native Bostonian and my

mother pure Irish. If anything, I got the Irish parts.'

'That's interesting — my father was American-Guyanian and my mother pure French. I got most of the French parts, so we're both a bit European!'

She nodded. That explained the shrug. She'd thought it almost looked French, and his gorgeous light brown complexion, brown eyes, aristocratic Gallic nose and wide mouth. She found it hard to believe the girls around the hospital had been able to leave him alone.

'Are your folks still alive?' he asked.

'My dad was killed in the line of duty. He was a cop. My mother got homesick and went back to Ireland. She lives in Dublin with her sister. I see her once or twice a year. We still have plenty of family there to take care of her, and I didn't want to leave America. You?'

'My dad was in the army and, like yours, died in service. My mother . . . ' Sam shook his head, and it seemed to her that for an instant a look of intense pain flitted over his features, then was gone. She didn't press it.

'That's a long story, Cindy, and some day I'll tell it to you, but here comes dinner.'

They ate slowly, enjoying the food, the wine, the restaurant, and most of all the company.

At 9.30, he said, reluctantly, 'I suppose we'd better go.'

She nodded, suddenly feeling unhappy that it was over.

As they drove through the outskirts of the city, Sam said, 'Cindy, that was the nicest evening I've had for a long time. Maybe we could do it again sometime?'

She didn't hesitate. 'Yes . . . please.' Some of the unhappiness was lifted from her.

He pulled up behind where she had parked the car.

'Shall we decide now? I feel bad calling your home.'

'Why not same time next week, if the duty rosters fit that?'

'OK. Unless either of us calls in different, same time, same place.'

She opened the door and then, as if she had forgotten something, leaned back towards him and brushed his cheek with a kiss so light it was as if a gentle spring breeze had touched him and was gone.

No words, no look back. She got into her car and drove off.

He noticed the bruise behind her ear was almost gone. He watched her drive away, then drove back to his Cambridge apartment, and walked in, enjoying the memories of the evening. He threw his jacket on the sofa, made himself some coffee and flicked on the TV.

'And on 22 November, a tribute to the memory of John F. Kennedy on the forty-second anniversary of his death entitled *Do You Remember?*'

Do you remember?

Sam Brown remembered. His enjoyment of the evening gave way to a sudden melancholy, and he lay back on the sofa, closing his eyes.

How could he ever forget the day Kennedy died . . .

5

August 1944

Richard Brown was a 28-year-old lieutenant in the US Army during the liberation of Paris. Nicole Duvalier was an 18-year-old Parisian girl. She was standing with the rest of the crowd on the Rue de Rivoli waving flags, whistling, cheering as the American tanks, armoured cars, and personnel carriers slowly drove past *en route* for the Champs-Elysées just as the German conquerors had five years before.

But this time to free Paris.

Some of the more adventurous girls threw roses to the soldiers, others jumped up on to the sides of the armoured cars and jeeps to hug or kiss the liberators. Nicole saw him coming from way back, the young, handsome, dark-skinned officer looking almost embarrassed by the process, not joining in the revelry as much as his colleagues. She fixed her eyes on him and, when his jeep drew level, she jumped on to the running board, threw her arms around his neck and kissed him on both cheeks. She felt his strong arm around her waist as he made sure she did not injure herself, then he let her slowly down on to the road, almost as if he did not want to let go. Her friends shrieked their approval and ran in her direction but Nicole stood, transfixed, oblivious of all around her, watching him go, their eyes locked together until he was out of sight. She half raised her hand to wave, before the attention and antics of her friends and the noise around them brought her back to reality.

Three days later, as she was walking across the Place de l'Opéra, three young GIs stopped to ask the way to Sacré Coeur. They prolonged the conversation with the pretty young French girl as long as possible, pretending not to understand her more than passable English, and were unaware of the presence of the officer until the authoritative voice enquired in perfect French, 'Are these men bothering you, miss?'

She recognized him immediately.

The three GIs sprang to attention.

'*Sir!*' barked one of them briskly.

'I wasn't talking to you, soldier, I was speaking to the young lady.'

She smiled. '*Pas du touts*' she replied.

'That's OK.' And in English, 'All finished here, soldiers?'

'Yes, *sir!*'

'At ease, and on your way then.'

The three young men saluted and hurried off in the direction Nicole had indicated, as the officer grinned to himself and turned to her.

'Hope I didn't break anything up there?'

She smiled again, shaking her head. They stood in silence for a few moments, before he asked, 'Would you care to walk a little?'

'Yes.'

So they walked back past Concorde, up the Champs-Elysée to look at the huge Tricolour which had been raised above the Arc de Triomphe, the first time such a flag had flown over Paris for a long time. Before they knew it, dusk was falling, and he walked her home.

'The city will be dangerous for some time,' he said, 'perhaps even more than before — trapped Nazis, communists, guerillas, nervous GIs — be careful. It will take many weeks to secure the peace here.'

She nodded. It had been dangerous for a long time but she saw his point.

'Would you be free at all tomorrow?' he asked. 'I have two days' leave.'

She nodded enthusiastically. Let the pâtisserie wait. 'It would be nice to show you our city, now it is free again,' she said.

And so they met each day, walking the Paris streets, Nicole showing Richard Brown the sights, Richard telling her of his Guyanian background, and his home in America.

On his last day, he stood before her in the small square outside the Church of St-Germain-des-Prés, and said, gently, 'Tomorrow I have to move south. I don't know when I will return to Paris.'

'I wonder if I will ever see you again?' she asked.

'Would you like to?'

She gave him a deep look that left him in no doubt of the answer. '*Oui*,' she whispered.

'*Moi, aussi*,' he replied, quietly. 'But I don't know when we will be back.'

'I understand.'

'If we are coming back, I will try to let you know. If I do, we'll meet here, outside the church' — he glanced at his watch — 'at noon. Or, if it is raining, over there in the Café de Trois Magots.'

She nodded.

They stood facing each other, neither wanting to leave. The square was bustling, people everywhere, but they ignored them all as he took her gently into his arms for the first time, and kissed her tenderly, on the lips, both of them lingering, oblivious of the world outside.

'I will see you again, Nicole,' he whispered, 'I promise.' Then, without a pause, he turned and walked away slowly, turning to wave every few paces, until he turned the corner and was gone.

She watched, feeling as if her heart might break.

During the weeks that followed she waited for letters, messages, but none came. She walked past the church at noon every day she was able and waited in vain.

She had almost given up hope when, two months later on a fine day, she walked up the Rue de Vaugirard on to the Boulevard St-Germain towards the church.

She saw the tall figure in the long trenchcoat immediately as he slowly paced the small square.

'Richard,' she whispered, then shouted, 'Richard,' and she began to run towards him.

He turned. 'Nicole!' he cried, and ran towards her, taking her into his arms, first kissing her then swinging her round and round.

They were married six months later.

Nicole had never imagined what life would be like as a military officer's wife, nor did she ever care. But by the time Samuel Richard was born, nine years later on 22 November 1954, just when his parents had thought they might never have a child, Nicole had already followed her husband, now with US Intelligence, on the disastrous French attempt to re-colonize Vietnam.

Here, his World War II experience and fluent French had been put to full use. Later, she watched from Washington as he went off to Korea, wondering once more if she would ever see him again. But she always did.

She knew these were dangerous missions, but knew also that her husband was immensely strong, sensible and courageous. By the time Sam was born, his father had a desk job in Washington DC, and Nicole took a six-month sabbatical from her position at the French Embassy, so that they were able to enjoy fully their new life.

There followed the happiest times of their life together: Richard with a secure post at the Pentagon, Nicole with a part-time post at the French Embassy, both of them watching their young child grow. When John F. Kennedy was elected to the White House in 1960, the family rejoiced. Now America could move on to greater things, particularly addressing the injustice and apartheid which afflicted the Southern States, and to which Richard Brown was bitterly opposed. So when, two years later, he was summoned to the Oval Office, and asked to help in a covert mission to make a detailed assessment of racial abuse in Alabama and Mississippi, a detail for which he was ideally equipped, he was flattered, and agreed without hesitation.

As usual, Nicole was supportive. At least he would be serving his country closer to home than on previous occasions — he would be only a short plane ride and a phone call away. At 3.30 p.m. on the afternoon of Friday, 22 November, 1963, Nicole was collecting Sam from school when the awful news began to drift in that President Kennedy had been assassinated by a sniper in downtown Dallas, Texas. She and her small son spent the rest of the afternoon glued to the TV, not believing what they were seeing and hearing. She half expected a call from Richard. At 6.30 precisely, there was a loud knock at the door. She went to answer it, reluctant to take her eyes off the TV screen. When she did open the door, two officers in army uniform were on the doorstep.

'Mrs Brown?'

She nodded, fear suddenly becoming an unwilling companion to the grief she was already feeling for the President.

'May we come in, please? I'm afraid we have some bad news for you.'

Richard's body had been found hanging in a Georgia wood beside the smouldering remains of what had been a flaming cross. His undercover mission had been rumbled by the Klan in that area, and he, and two of his three companions, had been murdered.

The officers were sympathetic and uncomfortable, as even the most professional bearers of such news invariably are.

Throughout the interview, young Sam stood silently beside his mother as she sat absorbing the news. She took it well, no tears being shed as the soldiers went through their reluctant duty. When it was over they rose and she saw them to the door. One of the officers paused, and leaned down to Sam.

'This has been a bad day for everyone, son. It's just you and your mom now. You take care of her.'

'*You take care of her . . .*'

Which is just what he had tried to do. Until . . .

A sudden change of programme on the TV roused Sam Brown from his reverie. He sighed, and cleared up before going to bed. As he waited for sleep, the words of Bobby Kennedy at the 1964 Democratic Convention came back to him. Talking of his brother, he quoted some lines from Shakespeare:

> *. . . When he shall die*
> *Take him and cut him out in little*
>   *stars,*
> *And he will make the face of heaven so*
>   *fine*

That all the world will be in love with
   night,
And pay no worship to the garish
   sun . . .

Then he remembered again the date: 22 November. His birthday. And the day two good men died.

6

Nick Bailey walked into The Nose Wine Bar on Boston's harbour front. It was a favourite with hospital staff especially the residents and nurses because of its busy informal atmosphere. The terrace outside with its tables and chairs facing the harbour was always the first to fill up when the weather was good. This evening it was empty, for the Boston nights were drawing in and there was a distinctly cool wind blowing from the Canadian north. The room he entered off the terrace was all natural wood: wooden floors, wooden walls and a large oak bar at the far end. To the side of the bar, a short corridor led to a larger bar with tables and chairs around the perimeter for drinkers and diners. Here, halfway up the wall the wood gave way to a warm green colour, matching the padded cushions of the chairs. A staircase led up to a third bar, also for diners.

He stopped at the bar in the first room.

'Large house red please,' he ordered. It was an Ernest and Julio Cabernet Sauvignon.

'Maybe I should buy that for you after what you went through the other night, Doctor?'

He turned to find Chris Hardy, the practitioner nurse standing behind him. He had not seen her out of the OR before and he almost dropped his wine with surprise. She was a tall girl with a tanned complexion, long very blonde hair and deep-brown eyes. But it was her lips that transfixed him. They were the fullest, most gorgeous, kissable lips he had ever seen. A vision of Marilyn Monroe flitted through his mind for that was the instant impression he got.

He coughed and said, 'Why thanks, Nurse Hardy. I'll take you up on that offer. But only if you let me get you one later.'

'It's a deal.'

They took their drinks to a table and sat down.

'Are you alone?'

'I was supposed to be meeting a girlfriend — Cindy James from OR — but she phoned just as I walked in the front door. Delayed at work. She might get here later. I saw you at the bar and decided to buy you a drink instead. Hope you don't mind. I'm not usually this forward.'

'No, it's really nice of you. I haven't had the chance to make many friends here yet. Cheers!'

'Cheers.' They clinked glasses. 'So, how are you enjoying Boston?'

'Apart from the other night, very much. It's a great city. Not sure I'll be able to survive winter though. We don't have winters like you get here back home in Melbourne.'

'I've heard it's pretty nice there too. Why did you leave?'

'Experience. Broaden the CV. This is a pretty good centre, and if I don't make too many cock-ups like the other night, I might get some good references from some very big names.'

'Like Sam Brown, for example?'

'Exactly. He's great, isn't he? Good gynaecologist, good surgeon, nice guy — he's got it all.'

'Sure has. We all fancy him but he doesn't seem interested in women. Not us anyway.'

'Doesn't mix business with pleasure maybe. Very wise.'

'Oh, yes? What do you think you're doing then, Dr Bailey?'

'Oh, we Aussies don't obey most of the rules. We always mix business with pleasure. Anyway, you are pretty irresistible out of the OR greens. Funny how different people look without their clothes.' He paused for a moment realizing what he had said. 'Oh, sorry . . . I mean . . . out of uniform . . . in different clothes . . . ' He blushed slightly thinking even Australians don't move that fast.

She laughed. 'I know what you mean.'

'I almost wouldn't have recognized you.'

'That's how it should be.'

'That was some case the other night, wasn't it?' he said, changing the subject.

'I've never seen anything like it before. We often see small bladder tears during a section, but they are just that, small, and the gynaecologists usually repair them themselves. I don't want to insult you but that was a whopper.'

'It sure was. She's doing great though. I've not had many problems with cases before. Although, I do remember the first cyst of the testicle that I ever removed. He was a big tough farmer from the outback. I was only a first-year trainee at the time. He bled afterwards and his scrotum filled up with blood until it was the size of a football. I had to take him back to theatre and drain it off. I was so concerned I went to see him three or four times every day for the next five days until he went home, just to check he was OK. Before he left he gave me a packet of cigars and told me he'd never been looked after so well in his life. I mean, it was my fault and he gave me cigars! These days I'd probably get a court summons for negligence!'

She laughed. 'You sure would. Especially here in the USA.'

'So what of you, Nurse Hardy? Do you have great nursing ambitions?'

'Not really, not for now anyway. I'm a urology practitioner nurse, a new post, and I'm loving it. I get to do clinics, flexible cystoscopies, bladder chemotherapy, all sorts. This is a two-month attachment to OBGYN. I've only been in post for six months and I need to get all the experience I can. Then maybe move on or move up depending on what's available.'

'Would you like to travel? Maybe come to Melbourne?'

'Why not? But I'm a Boston girl, born and bred. I think I'd miss it too much.'

'Well, if that's the case, Miss Boston girl, maybe you can show me around sometime? Show me the real Boston!'

She smiled. 'Nick, I'd really like that,' she said, enthusiastically. 'You're on. Next week-end?'

'Sure. I'm not on duty so that sounds good.'

They clinked glasses again. They had a date.

★   ★   ★

Peter Mendova drove out of the underground parking-lot of the Revere Building and made his way through the rush-hour traffic south on I95. He was pleased with his day. Four couples, two wanting AI treatment, one going straight for adoption. On the basis of probabilities that meant two, maybe three happy couples with new babies. And $100,000 in his bank account by the time they were processed.

He leaned back in his seat, recalling how Simone and he had planned their future, and how well it was turning out.

After their night of passion in New York, she had told him her story. She had been married for two years. Her husband was in computer software. They had planned to have a child early on before she pursued her career, but he was never able to do the job, and it transpired later that he was sterile. She was devastated: he didn't seem to care. He was more interested in bytes than babies. He left her eventually to pursue his own interests. She wondered what she had ever seen in him. The day she met Peter after their unsuccessful interviews, she was immediately attracted to him. Later, when they realized they were in love, she began to evolve her plans for their future. Plans she told him, she had been thinking about for some time but which he had catalysed for her. Plans which, as she described them to him, seemed not just possible, but positively achievable.

Once he had enthusiastically agreed to go forward with her, she arranged a semen analysis on him. The results were spectacular.

Volume: 6 ml; count: 200 million/ml; motility: 95%; abnormal forms: <5%.

Superman readings!

So, her plan unfolded. They would open an infertility clinic, do everything themselves, and undercut the expensive overheads of hospitals and pathology laboratories. Bend the rules. All they needed was premises, a supply of quality semen, laboratory and freezing facilities, and administration kits — of which the semen was the most important.

And they had that already: his.

Peter himself had his doubts about the possibility of cloning the world with little Mendovas until she explained it all to him — the cost of setting up a legitimate sperm bank, the problems they could expect from the authorities and, most important, what the profits from such a venture could be if they followed her suggestions. So they found the Revere building and took out a lease on the basis of their MD degrees. The realty company knew of no poor doctors in Boston, and the clinic duly opened.

Business started slowly, but with Simone's marketing and Peter's charm and confidence, things picked up so that they soon had their first success, a bonny bouncing boy for an overjoyed couple. Before long, the marketing, and word of mouth, assured a steady number of patients seeking their help. Peter was happy and, as usual, impressed with the determination and drive of his wife. However, he was soon to learn that complacency was not advisable when it came to Simone Belmont.

It was six months later when she decided on Plan B.

After looking carefully and seeing several realtors, she found an old mansion on the southern outskirts of the city, built in ten acres of land down a long drive off the main highway. They bought a three-year lease, moved in, and started to upgrade White Plains Estate.

One night, they were sitting on the veranda with a pitcher of wine when she came out with it. 'We need to move on, Peter, develop the service.'

'What do you mean?'

'We need babies.'

He looked at her, wondering what was coming next. She could see he wasn't with the idea.

'Babies, Peter. We make a good profit from the AI programme, especially when a baby results from it, but that's only a quarter of the cases. If we had a ready-made young baby, we could charge a bundle.'

'What do you mean, a ready-made young baby? Where on earth do we get that from? Steal one?'

'No. Make them. Using surrogates. And your semen.'

He looked exasperated. 'Simone, I'm just not following this. Who on earth will act as a surrogate? How do we advertise? How much do we pay them? And you know the risks of surrogates not wanting to hand over the babies once they are born. This is just too risky.'

He was feeling uncomfortable. The AI plan was a risk, could result in them being struck off the medical register, put them out of work. But surrogates?

'I know. If we were legit, we might advertise. But that sort of programme would attract too much attention and cost too much. So we need girls who are prepared to stay here for a few months as our guests, under our control — like a little community — and carry a pregnancy to term.'

He smiled. 'Like a sect? With us the spiritual leaders?' He laughed out loud at the concept.

Simone did not join in.

'Why not? It's been done a hundred times

before, though not for this reason.'

'And where are the girls coming from if we're not advertising?'

'We'll have to go out and get them. There are enough bombed-out, drifting junkies on the streets of the city to entice here. Promise them food, shelter, drugs, then get them to stay.'

'They wouldn't though.'

'Oh wouldn't they? Do you remember at med school, during the psychiatry module, learning about wartime brainwashing? The CIA protocol? Solitary confinement, disorientation programmes, hypnosis. Add in diazepam and temazepam, a little methadone, plenty of grass, a little crack occasionally, and the promise of five thousand dollars when the baby is born. That might be an improvement on street life.'

'And how do we get them here? Kidnap them?'

She smiled. 'Exactly.'

Now he really looked shocked. 'But that's a federal offence. If we were caught . . . '

'We won't be, Peter. We'll be taking a poor young addict off the streets and giving her a home. After a short time, she'll never remember how she got here. She'll be under long-term hypnosis and drugs, and will be completely dependent on us. And when another girl joins her, the community begins.

And as the babies start arriving we rotate them out again. Then everyone's happy.'

He took a lot of convincing this time. Cloning childless women with his own semen was one thing, but Simone was becoming outrageous. He had a lot of doubts about the wisdom of really going over the top and kidnapping people, but Simone kept on and on at him until he began to waver, and eventually agreed to at least go out in the car and scout around a little. They found the first girl semi-comatose on a bench on Beacon Hill at two in the morning. When Peter approached her, she told him in a slurred voice it would cost fifty dollars. He walked her to the car for the blow job she was expecting to give him for her next fix, only to find Simone waiting there. Peter held her while Simone expertly slid in the intravenous medazolam, and within seconds she was snoring. Later, Simone extracted the information that she was a drifter, living on the streets. No family contacts, no one expecting her home. Within three weeks, Leanne was the most content, obedient 17-year-old in Boston. They redesigned the first floor into four secure apartments and within another six months, two more were occupied. Three girls, HIV negative, in a pleasant, hypnotic, secure home, like zombies.

Pregnant zombies. Members of the Mendova Sect.

He smiled as he remembered the progress they had made over the past eighteen months. He turned off I93 on to Dorchester Avenue. Twenty minutes later, he reached the huge wrought-iron gate protecting the estate and clicked the security remote. The gate creaked open slowly. Whoever had owned this house had been security conscious, and that suited Peter and Simone very well indeed. They didn't want anyone snooping into their business, or speaking to their girls. He gave a sigh of contentment as he got out of the car.

Good old Simone, he thought to himself. She's always right.

7

Nick and Chris met as planned on the steps of the Boston Public Library, Nick creeping up behind her then putting his hands over her eyes.

She screamed, then realized from his laugh it was him.

'Nick, don't do that! It frightened me!'

'C'mon, takes more than that to frighten a urological practitioner nurse, surely? So, where are we going?'

She took his hand and started to walk.

'We'll start at Copley,' she said, 'then take it from there.'

So they walked first to Copley Square, one of Boston's finest downtown areas, and across to the plush Copley Plaza Hotel where Chris treated him to coffee. Then it was across the square to the Hancock Tower.

'Hell,' he said, staring up, 'this is impressive.'

'Boston's tallest building,' she said proudly. 'Even better from the top.'

They walked in to the elevators. Within a couple of minutes they were sixty floors up at the top staring out over the city and its

68

environs. She pointed out the landmarks, Boston Bay, Logan Airport, Quincy to the south, the Charles River and Cambridge to the west, Revere to the north. Boston Common 'the oldest park in the country,' she said proudly. It was a fine day and the view was excellent.

They had a late lunch at the Boston Oyster Bar, and spent the afternoon walking around the waterfront before dragging themselves to The Nose at about 6.30.

A glass of wine later, Nick leaned back in his chair with his hands behind his head and said, 'Well, Chris, that was one hell of a day. I feel like I know your Boston an awful lot better than I did this morning.'

'Me, too! I love doing that walk. So what now?'

He looked at her and she returned the look without blinking.

'Well, now that we know Boston, maybe we might get to know each other a little? Why don't we have a few tapas here and a little more wine, then decide in which apartment we spend the evening together. It's been such a great day, I don't want it to end.'

She leaned over the table until their faces were just a couple of inches apart and whispered, 'That sounds pretty good to me, Dr Bailey.'

The following Tuesday, Sam Brown and Cindy met as planned, a week after their first dinner. They followed the same routine exactly, except that this time there was little of the original nervousness. Cindy had been looking forward to the evening all week and her natural affection for the gynaecologist allowed her to slip into a relaxed mood with him faster than she could have thought possible. In any case, all her nervousness had been dissipated during the operating list after their first meeting. She had had to concentrate very hard indeed to maintain the standard of which Sam had expressed approval but, once she got into her stride, professionalism and training took over and, before long, she found herself enjoying the cases. If anyone noticed a slightly relaxed atmosphere around the table compared to normal, no one commented on it.

The meal was excellent and they lingered a little longer than the first time, talking about everything and anything as people do when first they begin a relationship. This time when they parted at the end of the evening, the kiss was more substantial, and so warm and complete that she would have gone anywhere with him had he asked at that moment. But she left him again, fighting her instincts lest she might spoil things, only this time, as she opened the door of her car, she turned and gave a small wave. He returned it, as if he had been waiting for it.

She was parking the car outside her home by eleven, surprised to see the house lights on. Billy was not usually home before one on a Tuesday.

She opened the door warily, expecting trouble, but before she had gone far she heard the familiar snores from the living-room. She went quietly to the bathroom, then tiptoed to the bedroom, sliding into the king-size bed, praying that he would snore until dawn, by which time she would be up and preparing to leave for work. She fell into a light sleep. It must have been three when she heard noises indicating he was awake. Usually he would go to the bathroom then back to the sofa knowing her reaction if he tried to crawl drunk into bed beside her, but tonight the noises and movements were heading towards the bedroom and not the living-room. She pulled the sheet up under her chin and feigned sleep, hoping he would return to the living-room, but her worst fears were realized when the light went on and the sheet was ripped away from her, leaving her naked on the bed.

'So, where have you been tonight, my darling wife? Out with the girls? Or the boys maybe?' She sensed rather than saw the lunge towards her and leapt off the other side of the bed, grabbing her robe from the chair, and running around the foot of the bed as he lurched across it, falling in his residual drunkenness over the other side. She made for the kitchen, grabbing for the drawer to get the knife. She knew she was in danger, that he would hurt her again, but this time she was not prepared to tolerate it. She pulled open the drawer, screaming in agony as it was slammed shut against her fingers. She turned towards him just as the blow exploded in her eye and she felt herself losing consciousness and falling to the floor, leaving her hand trapped in the drawer above her as he shrieked his crazed obscenities; then everything went dark.

She had no idea how long she was unconscious. The first thing she was aware of was the inability to open her right eye. She wondered where she was for a moment before the pain in her right hand and the blurred memories of events arrived simultaneously. She groaned involuntarily as she moved to get up, listening for evidence that he might still be close, ready to beat her some more, but the apartment was quiet. She crawled up the side of the kitchen units until she was able to stand, then walked unsteadily to the bathroom. She recoiled when she saw her face in the mirror. Her eye was closed entirely by the trauma of the blow, the eyelid red, and swollen to twice its normal size, and there was a cut over her eyebrow, concealed beneath a clot of dried blood. She looked down at her hand. The fingers were swollen and bruised, but she could at least open and close them, albeit with pain. She listened again for sounds, but the apartment was quiet. He had probably gone out to his usual bar where he often drank till dawn. She realized that this time she could no longer stay in the house. He was getting increasingly violent, and now she had had two bad beatings, the last being a real threat to her. She had to do something about the situation before he killed her. Or she killed him. She went to the kitchen and took some ice from the fridge, wrapping it in a towel and holding it against her eye as she sat at the kitchen-table, quietly weeping to herself.

She cleaned herself up as best she could, took a shower, and dressed, then picked up the phone and pushed some numbers. It was several rings before her friend answered in a sleepy voice.

'Chrissy, it's me, Cindy. Sorry, I know it's

late but I need some help. Can I come over?'

Fifteen minutes later, the cab deposited her outside Chris Hardy's apartment. She paid the driver, grabbed her case and walked up to the door, pushing the bell.

Chris gasped when she saw her friend. 'My God, Cindy, what happened? Come in; here, give me the bag.'

Cindy closed the door and followed her into the living-room where she slumped gratefully on to the couch. Her friend sat beside her.

'Billy?'

Cindy nodded.

'God, you're a mess, girl. You should be down in ER not here.'

'No!' Cindy almost shouted the word, then looked apologetically at Chris through her good eye. 'Sorry, I can't. I'm OK, really.'

'All right, but let me take a look at you.'

She checked the eye, gently lifting the lid to check the underlying eyeball.

'Can you see me?' she asked.

'Yes.'

She then inspected the laceration, before turning to the hand, feeling the fingers, checking for fractures or tendon injury, insisting that her friend open and close, then spread her fingers before placing her index and middle fingers in the palm of her hand

and making her squeeze them.

'Any other injuries, Cindy? Did he kick you? Any abdominal trauma?'

Cindy shook her head slowly.

'Right,' she said, rising from the sofa. 'I'm going to get some spirit for that cut and a cold compress for your eye. Then I'm going to fix us each a large brandy while you tell me what's going on and what we're going to do about it.'

★   ★   ★

It was about 8.30 when Peter Mendova walked into the house, dropped his attaché case on the kitchen floor and mixed himself a strong vodka-tonic. Simone was waiting for him in the drawing-room. She kissed him passionately, then sat on the sofa, indicating that he should do likewise. Her look suggested that his pleasure was about to be interrupted.

'What is it? What's wrong?'

'We might have a problem, Pete.'

'What sort of problem?'

'Do you remember when the first baby was born and then sold at six weeks? It seemed to work fine separating him from Leanne immediately, then allowing Leanne, Jenny and Lorene to share him. It gave them a sense of family, and it gave Leanne some pride in what she'd done. It's really quite astounding how these poor kids have accepted their purpose, their new life. Oh sure, the hypnosis and the drugs help them forget, lose time, accept everything. But it's all working better than I ever thought it could.'

'So what's wrong?'

'Jenny.'

He moved away from her slightly, turning his head to face her. 'Jenny?'

She nodded.

'But she's only a month away from delivery. What's wrong?'

'She's becoming attached to the baby. Talking about wanting to keep it.'

'How do you know?'

'She spoke to Leanne.'

He looked concerned now. 'How has it happened? Not enough temazepam? Not susceptible to hypnosis? I hadn't noticed anything different about her.'

'I don't know. Maybe she has a basic maternal instinct overriding the drugs. Perhaps she came from a strong family background. Maybe her lifetime ambition has been to be a mother. Whatever, we need to handle it. If she starts blabbing to Lorene, she could spread doubts, stir up resentment.'

'Should we isolate her?'

76

Simone looked at him with a cold, fixed stare. 'If she doesn't respond to therapy in the next couple of weeks, we might have to isolate her completely. There's too much to lose, now things are really beginning to move.'

'You mean dump her back on the streets?'

'Whatever it takes, Peter.'

Peter Mendova returned her look, not fully understanding what she was suggesting, not really wanting to. As fast as realization dawned on him, he banished the thought from his mind. He nodded acquiescence, even as he began the process of mental denial. That had always been his way. If something frightened or worried him, he would simply pretend it did not exist, and blunder on until it went away, or he could no longer hide from the consequences. Simone was the organizer. She would sort matters out.

'Whatever you say,' he said.

'I'll watch her over the next week. Leanne will help; she knows the rules. We'll see how it goes. Either way, she must have the baby. The kid's worth a lot: she's worth nothing.

8

The surgeons' room was full. Urology was represented by Jerry Weinberg and his resident Humberto Testa; gynaecology had Professor Dan Peters and Nick Bailey; neuro-surgery had Bill Connor and his resident, and orthopaedics brought up the rear with Jerry Lydon. It was usually a noisy room, the surgeons swapping experiences, discussing politics of the hospital and national variety, or discussing cases of mutual interest.

Today the room was silent. All eyes were on the TV where details of a horrific murder in the city were being relayed. They listened to the dialogue in disbelief.

'It is thought the bodies had been there for some time, possibly over a week. The male has been identified as Michael Thomas, a thirty-two-year-old Afro-American legal adviser. The female victim was his long-time girlfriend Sue Lever, who was a local white girl. She had been violently assaulted and raped, then strangled. Her boyfriend had been tied up and beaten, then had his neck broken. Their bodies were hidden in undergrowth in the Back Bay Fens park. A note was found pinned to his chest. It read: *From the Kleagle, on behalf of the Imperial Wizard and the Emperor. Twice has the serpent hissed. When again his voice is heard your doom is sealed.*

The reporter looked up from his notes.

'It seems,' he said seriously, yet in an almost disbelieving voice, 'it seems that we have a Klan problem in Boston.'

The surgeons looked at each other in horror as the picture faded from the screen and the network returned to the studio.

★   ★   ★

Later that day, Nick and Chris were sitting in bed together in his apartment, eating cheese and biscuits, sipping wine and listening to Luther: *Buy me a rose.* The ultimate in truly emotional romance.

After their Boston tour, they had gone back to her place and the lovemaking that followed was as natural, easy and beautiful as either of them could have expected. As soon as they walked through the door, they had faced each other and slowly, so slowly, embraced, their lips meeting, gently at first, then more firmly, their tongues slowly exploring until they both felt the passion rising and knew what must happen next. She broke away and, taking his hands, backed slowly towards the bedroom, looking once more directly into his eyes. Once there, they kissed again as she undid his belt and zipper, then knelt to remove his trousers and shorts, lingering there for a moment to take him slowly deep into her mouth, to show him what he might expect, to demonstrate that he was special. He groaned with pleasure as she left him, to stand up and take off his shirt as she faced him again. He picked her up and carried her to the side of the bed where he lifted her dress over her head, undid her bra and very gently kissed her breasts, sucking on the nipples until she felt they might burst. He slipped her panties off and she lay back on the bed, as his tongue once more caressed her breasts, then her stomach moving down to her very being as he repaid the compliment, stimulating her desire, showing her with gentle confidence that she was special too, and he was not going to rush or spoil the moment. Eventually he worked his way up to her lips, and she felt his stunning erection and guided it into her with a gasp of pleasure.

They both knew that was no one-night stand, and the lovemaking this evening had been just as special and wonderful as that first time.

'Hell, Chris, I'm so glad we got together,' he said. 'You're fantastic.'

'You're not so bad yourself, Mr Oz. It was meant to happen.' She sighed a sigh of pure satisfaction and snuggled her head into his shoulder.

'How's your friend Cindy?' he asked, remembering what she had told him earlier on.

'She's OK. But that bastard husband of hers has beaten her for the last time. It's been going on for months, years maybe, but she just stuck it out from some ingrained Catholic fidelity. And after what I said about your Dr Brown, he's been really good to her, supported her through it.'

'Ah ha,' said Nick, mischievously. 'Mixing business with pleasure?'

She nudged him in the ribs almost causing him to spill the wine.

'No, there's been no hanky panky; he's just been there for her. Maybe they like each other more than we know. Like we said, Sam's a good guy, and Cindy, Christ, she deserves a bit of good news for a change.'

He nodded. Sam Brown could do no harm in his eyes.

'Well, let me know if I can be of any help,' he said, and they clinked glasses, just like they had in The Nose a few days earlier, before they got to know each other.

★ ★ ★

'Pete! Pete, wake up quickly; she's gone!'

Peter Mendova sat bolt upright in the bed, rubbing his eyes, wondering what was happening. He felt his shoulders being shaken.

'Pete! For God's sake, Jenny's gone!'

He looked into Simone's eyes, realization of what she was saying sinking in.

'Gone? Gone where? When?'

'I don't know. Leanne just called to say she saw her at ten o'clock but she was disturbed by noises at twelve. When she went to investigate, Jenny was gone.'

Peter leapt out of bed, grabbing for his clothes. 'Shit! What time is it now?'

'Twelve thirty. I can't find her around here. She can't have got far.'

'Unless she's taken one of the cars.'

'She couldn't.'

'Any clue where she's headed?'

'Well, it can only be north or south from here if she's heading for the freeway.'

'OK, I'll take the Lexus and head south. You take the Jeep and go north. Simone, what if she won't come back?'

She paused, looking at him. She had not considered that.

'She'll have to, even if we have to force her. There's a gun in the Lexus glove compartment — that should frighten her.'

'And if she's not frightened?'

'We'll take the medicine bags too, there's hypnoval and diazepam already drawn up. This baby's important to us, Pete. In fact, the whole project is important to us. I'm not going to see it wrecked by some worthless street junkie. If she talks . . . '

'You're right. So let's just get her back, one way or the other. We'll sort out details later. Are the others secured?'

Simone nodded as they ran to the garage.

They got into the cars and sped down the drive and through the gate where Pete turned south in the Lexus and Simone north in the Jeep. She was seething with anger. She should have spotted this coming, put a guard on Jenny as soon as she started talking out of turn, given her more sedatives, done something . . . anything.

She raced along the quiet road, but after a

mile there was still no sign of Jenny. She reached the T-junction where the roads led north to Boston, and south to Rhode Island. She went north, speeding along the highway. Then, she saw her, walking slowly along the side of the road, thumb out, trying to hitch a ride. The only car to pass her flew by without stopping, but she saw the Harley Davidson's brake lights go on as it slowed down, and sensed what would happen.

'Shit,' she said out loud, 'the biker's going to stop.'

Which he did.

Simone slowed down also, thinking fast. Her options were limited now. She checked the rearview mirror. No traffic behind. None ahead.

She took a deep breath and pressed her foot down firmly on the accelerator pedal, gathering speed towards the biker and the pregnant girl who was looking gratefully at the biker as he stopped beside her. Neither of them suspected what was happening until she was almost upon them. Then, just for a moment, Jenny turned, seeming for a split second to recognize Simone before the Jeep hit the biker, the bike and her at the same time. The Jeep went right over the biker, hitting the girl directly and throwing her up over the bonnet to fall behind the speeding

Jeep. Simone braked hard, screeching to a halt, her eyes scanning the road for traffic. There wasn't any.

She did a U-turn, driving slowly towards them. Jenny was lying at the side of the road, her neck twisted at a bizarre angle. The biker and his vehicle were in the middle of the road. For a moment she thought she saw his head move. Was he still alive? Had he made the make and registration? At the last moment as she approached him, she turned the wheel and felt the bump as the 4×4 went over his head. Make and registration deleted, she thought, as once more she stood on the accelerator pedal and roared away from the scene. Thirty seconds later, she slowed as she spotted the lights of an oncoming truck. He would raise the alarm, she thought. But by then, it would be too late.

She soon reached home and drove straight into the garage killing the engine and jumping out to inspect the damage. There was surprisingly little. The bull bar was bent and would need to be removed, and there were a few scratches and bloodstains on the near-side fender, but nothing that could not be righted easily to cover up the events of the night.

She went into the kitchen, locking the garage behind her. She would see to the Jeep later. It was an hour before Peter returned, running into the kitchen, an anxious look on his face.

'Did you find her?' he asked, breathlessly.

She got up and went to him, giving him a hug.

'Yes, Peter, everything's OK. There was an auto wreck on the Boston road. I'm afraid she's dead. But at least she won't be able to harm us.'

'Dead, oh no, that's terrible.'

He seemed truly concerned, which made her angry.

'Peter!' she snapped. 'Dead is better than alive in the DA's office telling him about us! For Christ's sake, get real on this.'

He looked at her, nodding slowly, accepting her logic. 'What happened?' he asked, sheepishly.

'I don't know. Looked like she got picked up by a biker and got a hit-and-run. There was a truck there and the cops and UHSM medics arrived at the same time. I passed them by, and took a diversion home. She looked pretty dead though.'

'What a waste.'

'Well, yes. And fifty thousand bucks.'

'Simone, she's dead for Christ's sake.'

'She could have blown the next half-million bucks.'

He nodded glumly. 'We'll have to look at the medication regime. Something's not right if this sort of thing can happen. We need total control.'

'Yes, you're right. We'll just have to write this one off as experience and make sure it doesn't happen again. I'll explain everything to Leanne and we'll talk about what to do in the evening when you get in. This was a close call.'

He was beginning to feel better about it. Things had been resolved. Simone was in control. Shame about Jenny, but they had an objective and nothing should stand in their way. Good old Simone. Always sorts things out.

★   ★   ★

Billy James sat slumped in the chair, trying to focus on the screen. Headline News was reporting on the double killings in the Boston area. In his stupor he had managed to learn that some madman was tracking down white girls going out with black guys, and bumping them off. Some sort of racist or Ku Klux Klan maniac. In his drunken state, Billy was beginning to think that sounded like a very good idea. He took another swig of bourbon and looked around the living-room. It was littered with empty bottles, cans, fast food junk, newspapers. She had been gone three days now and he had returned just that day to find she'd sneaked back to collect her stuff.

'Bitch!' he shouted. He shut one eye and squinted again at the screen. Was *she* with a black guy? A doctor? Maybe the Boston killer would find her and save him the trouble. But there was no guarantee of that. He would have to go looking for her, find her and whoever she was shacked up with, and teach them both that it doesn't pay to mess with Billy James. Oh no. The thought seemed to sober him a little, and he began to plan it in his mind. He would go to the hospital, wait for her in the parking-lot, follow her, wait until he caught them together, then give them both a good beating. Or better still, kill them both. He had a gun in the house somewhere, and he could use it. Oh yeah, he'd once been one of the better shots in the department. And maybe they'd think it was the double killer. Especially if he raped her too. After all, that was what the killer was doing. Fucking the white girl, then killing them both. And it had been at least a year since he'd fucked her.

Or anything else, for that matter.

He got up and stood staring into space, the bottle hanging from his left hand, his right hand outstretched like it was holding a gun.

'Bam! Bam!' he cried, laughing out loud. 'And it's another hit for the Boston Killer.' Oh yeah! Now was the time. There'd never be a better alibi. He would show the little Irish whore that she'd gone too far this time.

'I'm coming, bitch.' he yelled, laughing at his own joke. 'Oh yes, I'm coming.'

9

The pager went off just as Sam Brown was parking in the staff lot. He glanced at the clock on the dashboard. It showed 06.05. He had just two hours to go of his night-time emergency on-call shift for OBGYN. The screen showed 3232: ER.

He decided it would be quicker to go straight there rather than waste time stopping to call. If ER asked for OBGYN it usually meant something pretty serious. He got out of the car and flicked the security button, walking quickly away to the screech of the activated alarm.

The nurse at reception saw him arrive. 'Resus, Dr Brown,' she called. He nodded and made for the bay used for the resuscitation of critical cases. He saw the ER team surrounding the trolley on which lay the unconscious naked body of a young pregnant girl lying amidst the detritus of attempted cardiopulmonary massage. Nick Bailey was completing his examination.

'What've you got, Nick?' Sam asked.

Nick looked up. 'Jane Doe, young caucasian female brought in an hour ago. A four by four hit her and a biker head on up off I95 somewhere. It seems she was thumbing a lift. Hit and run. She's got a stove-in chest, bilateral pneumothorax, multiple fractures. She's brain dead, Dr Brown. But she's also pregnant almost to term. Foetal heart present. She's intubated and ventilated on a hundred per cent oxygen and her cardiac output is OK. We can't save her, but maybe the baby . . .'

He stopped as he saw Sam taking a stethoscope from one of the nurses and bending over to listen to the heart beating within the dying uterus. It did not sound entirely normal.

'We need to prep for an instant C-section. Can we move her to the OR?'

'Sure but — '

Nick's reply was punctuated by the blip-blip of the monitor changing suddenly to an insistent, continuous high-pitched tone.

'She's arrested!' yelled the emergency room resident, immediately starting cardiac massage.

'Scalpel, someone!' Sam took off his jacket and threw it to the floor, and a nurse held out a number 9 blade.

Sam shoved an intern aside and without hesitation made a ten-inch transverse incision over the lower part of the pregnant abdomen.

The team had paused momentarily, but started up again as Nick shouted 'Carry on, guys, keep up the blood supply to the baby till it's born.' A second flash of the scalpel opened the uterus and Sam inserted his size 8½ hand into the womb, virtually scooping out the tiny baby girl.

'Clamp!'

It was in his hand in an instant and he clamped the cord. A tiny cry split the air as he cut the cord and the whole team suddenly felt a small pang of triumph.

'OK, everyone, relax,' said the ER resident, stepping back from the body, glancing at the clock.

He switched off the respirator, turning down the monitor bleep so they wouldn't have to listen to the depressing sound of the inevitable.

'Time of death seven thirty,' he announced quietly.

'Same as the time of birth,' muttered Sam, grimly, handing over the tiny baby to a nurse holding out a blanket. 'Has anyone called paeds? This baby needs some help.'

'They're on the way,' replied the nurse, who had taken the baby.

'Could someone put some tension sutures into the mother's abdomen?' Sam called over his shoulder, as he washed his hands at the resus scrub-up area. 'I don't want her going down to the morgue in that state.'

'I'll do it, Dr Brown,' said Nick, nodding to the scrub nurse to get the sutures.

As soon as the paediatrician arrived, Sam picked up his jacket and walked to the ER office to complete the paperwork. His shirt was covered in blood, and he realized he would have to go home and change. He called his secretary and left a message for her to put back his appointments to ten, finished the paperwork, and left ER for the parking-lot. What a start to the day, he thought to himself, feeling a mixture of accomplishment that the baby was OK, and sadness that it should enter its life at the very instant its young mother left hers. On his way through the Boston traffic, his thoughts turned to Cindy James. He had not seen her for several days, and had not heard anyone explaining her absence from the OR. He wondered if he should call her, then put the thought out of his mind. She was, after all, a married woman whom probably he should not be seeing anyway. He decided to give it a few more days.

Two days later, Sam was working in his office when the phone rang. It was John Reader, the chief of paediatrics.

'Sam, just thought I'd call to let you know

progress with the Jane Doe baby if you haven't already seen it on local TV. She's a little on the thin side, slightly jaundiced, but generally in pretty good shape. You got her out before she got anoxic. Good job you were on hand. Oh, and she's got Holt-Oram syndrome, although that shouldn't be too much of a problem.'

'That's good news, John. Except the last bit — Holt-Oram? Isn't that a hole in the heart?'

'Yes, an atrial septal defect, associated with a short thumb. A slight developmental glitch at the fifth week of gestation, when the septum between the right and left atria and the upper limb are both developing. It's not life threatening, although she may need surgery later.'

'Well, thanks again, John. Glad to hear she made it against all odds.'

He replaced the handset wondering what the future would be for the little sprite he had plucked so unceremoniously from her mother, thinking again of the synchronous birth and death. And what would be her fate now? She would move from ICU to the children's unit, then become a ward of court, to be fostered and eventually put up for adoption. Unless a relative came forward, a parent, a sibling even, to claim and care for her. The biker had ID, but he was from

Mississippi with no recorded next of kin. All the gear they found was male stuff, so she must have been hitching a ride into the city. But from where? He shook his head. What was the name of that cop who had worked on a couple of cases in the hospital over the past year or two? Joe Kennedy, that was it. Hopefully he might get involved and find something out, but he had a sneaky feeling little baby Doe was an orphan now.

Orphan Annie, he thought, unconsciously giving her a name. He stood up and put on his white coat.

'I'm going to the operating room, Rosemary,' he called to his secretary. Halfway there he met Jerry Weinberg.

'Hey Sam, hear you did a neat bit of emergency work down in ER last week.'

'Just routine stuff in the life of a gynaecologist, Jerry. Not as dull a life as you plumbers have, you know.'

'Oh sure, tell me about it.' Jerry stopped, becoming serious suddenly. 'Sam, did you hear about Senator Kingston? He was a friend of yours, I think?'

'A sort of friend. I met him at a few fund-raising events. He's a good man. Presidential stuff — could be the first black president some day. Why? What about him?'

'He's dead, Sam. Him and his wife. There's

a killer out there possibly picking on black men with white wives. Some grudge thing. They're both dead.'

'My God.' Sam was truly shocked. What a waste of two good people. Two wonderful people who could have made such a difference to their country. 'I'm truly shocked, Jerry. How did you hear?'

'Breaking news on CNN just as I left the office. I can't believe it myself. And the police haven't got a clue about the perp. Not a clue. Second case — there was another couple murdered a few weeks back. It was all over the TV.'

They walked on in silence, until Sam turned into the OR with a 'later' to Jerry. This was turning into a bad week, he thought to himself. Jesse Kingston was one of those rare individuals who only comes along once in a lifetime. Like JFK. A genuinely talented man of the people. He changed into his scrubs and walked into the operating room pulling on his cap. Cindy James was laying out the instruments for the first case. She glanced at him then returned quickly to her work.

'Morning, everyone,' said Sam. 'Just a hyst and a colpo this morning, so it should be an early lunch if we're lucky.'

He had already noticed the resolving bruise around Cindy's eye, in spite of her attempts to disguise it with make-up and by pulling her cap down low and her mask up high. Sam scrubbed up and walked to the table as the porter and anaesthetist wheeled in the patient.

'How are you, Nurse James? Nice to see you back,' he said nonchalantly, without even looking at her.

'I'm fine, thank you, Doctor.'

They started the case. He remembered their dinner together at the Cape, and the bruise behind her ear, also disguised by a scarf and make-up. There was only one explanation for these kinds of injuries and he had to talk to her about it. The second case came and went with the usual banter between surgeon, anaesthetist and nurses until Sam was finished.

'Thank you, everyone,' he said. 'See you Thursday.'

As the staff dispersed to clear up he walked close to Cindy on his way out and whispered 'Call me' without knowing if she had heard him.

The rest of the day passed in a routine fashion. He saw several patients in his office after lunch, and later called in the ICU to see Orphan Annie.

It was after seven when he got home. He threw his case on to the sofa and made for the kitchen fridge for a beer. The phone rang before he could open the can.

'Sam Brown.'

There was a momentary silence before she spoke. 'Sam, it's Cindy.'

'Cindy, where are you? Can we meet? Are you OK?'

She laughed. 'Didn't you once say to me one question at a time, Doctor?'

'Huh? Oh, sure, but — '

'I'm at a friend's house in the city. I don't want her to see us together.'

'That's OK. Give me the address; I'll pick you up outside.'

They arranged to meet outside Le Bon Pain down the road from Chris's apartment. He was there in twenty minutes, pulling over sharply when he saw her, ignoring the exasperated horn from the Hess truck behind.

She got in and he moved off immediately, doing a U-turn at the next junction and heading back in the direction he had come from.

'Where are we going?' she asked.

'Back to my place. Did you eat?'

'I'm not hungry. Is it OK to go to your place?'

'Sure. I never see my neighbours. We're not under surveillance. We can talk there.' He gave her a quick glance. 'You OK?'

'Sure. Well, kind of.'

'I wasn't sure you'd call; I've been worried.'

'I almost didn't. But I needed to see you.'

There. It was said, and she didn't regret it.

'Me, too. I almost called your house a few times but it wouldn't have been right.'

'I wasn't there anyway.'

The car sped over the Charles River to Cambridge as they continued talking. Within a few minutes they were there.

'Come on in, I'll show you around.'

She was impressed. The small hallway led to a huge living-room, with a kitchen and dining area behind it. A separate dining-room had been converted into a study. There were two *en suite* bedrooms.

'What can I get you?' he asked, as she sat down on the sofa.

'A Coke would be fine.'

'Sure? I've got Bud Ice, or a bottle of Sutter Home Merlot begging to be opened.'

She smiled, remembering the Cape. 'Sutter Home.'

When he brought the drinks he sat on the matching sofa opposite hers, the coffee-table between them and studied her face.

'Does he beat you often?' he asked gently.

For a moment she almost denied it, was about to make up some lame excuse, before she nodded, looking down into her glass, almost ashamed to admit it, as if it were her fault.

'You called the police.'

It was more of a statement than a question but she shook her head and said 'No.'

He looked incredulous. 'No? Why not?'

'I'm still thinking it through. Don't worry, my friend Chrissy took pictures.'

'That may not be enough, Cindy. Did you go to the ER?'

'No.'

'So there's no hospital record, no police record. He'd probably get off scot free now even if you did report it. Do you love him?'

She stared at him and he stared back, shifting in his seat, realizing he had no right to go on at her this way.

'Sorry,' he said quietly, 'it's just that I want to help . . . '

'I know,' she said. 'I've left him for good. Chris will put me up till I find a place. We went back to the house when Billy was out and I got my things. I've got enough saved to live on. I was the bread winner anyway. He's on a small pension which keeps him in booze. It's him who'll have the problem. And I've made an appointment to see an attorney.'

He relaxed a little. She had a game plan.

'Well, anything I can do to help, you only

have to ask. Money, a place to stay, professional contacts.'

'Thanks, Sam. God, I feel so *ashamed*. Me, a beaten wife. How have I let this happen?'

She tried to stem the tears but they came anyway. He moved across to sit with her, putting his arm around her so that she snuggled into his huge shoulder, burying her face in his chest. It was over in a moment.

'Sorry,' she said, wiping her eyes, and brushing a little mascara from his shirt, only making it streak more. She took a tissue from her pocket, blew her nose, and attempted a smile. 'There, all better.'

'Do you want to talk about it?'

'Not really. There's not much to talk about. He was a good-looker way back. We got together, I got pregnant, he married me, and the baby was stillborn. That hurt him, then he got caught by a bullet at a shootout and was pensioned off on health grounds. He had no other interests, started drinking more and more, then, for the last six months, started beating on me. He'd always roughed me up a little. Irish cop — master of the house — but it got really bad during the past few months. I had to threaten him with a knife twice to get away. This last one was the worst though.' She felt her eye gingerly.

'This time I knew it was the end. I think I

only stayed with him because of the Catholic background. For better for worse. Fine. Up to a point. But I realize now all I did was work, clean, cook, get roughed up a little, give him drinking money, then start the cycle over again. He did me a favour this time. Gave me the exit route.'

She looked at him, a long, lingering look, and whispered, 'It's over.'

They sat there for a while, then Sam got up, flicked on the CD, filled their glasses, and went to the kitchen. She sat sipping the merlot, listening to Fleetwood Mac until he returned with a plate of Camembert, tomatoes with oil and basil, celery and grapes. It didn't last long.

'I thought you weren't hungry,' he said, grinning.

'So did I,' she laughed.

She insisted on doing the dishes while he made coffee.

'What next?' he asked, eventually.

'File for divorce, make a new life, start over.'

'Can I help?'

'You are helping, Sam. Chris and you were the only people I could turn to over this, and I hardly know you at all. But we must be careful. If Billy knows about you, suspects you and I are . . . well . . . are friends, then he might blame you, cite you as the cause of the break-up, and get away with it. I couldn't take that, Sam, dragging you into this sordid business; apart from the fact that he could win. And the thought of your name being in the papers, people at work gossiping, I couldn't stand that.'

'I know. But please let me help if I can. Let me be a friend.'

'Oh I will, Sam, I will. I want you to be more than a friend, believe me.'

He looked at her, believing what she said, realizing he was feeling the same way.

'It's the same for me, Cindy,' he said. 'Things will be different one day, and when they are, I'll be here.'

She snuggled into him and they sat together for a while until she glanced at her watch, sat up and said, 'I've got to go, Sam. Sorry.'

'That's OK, Cindy, but tell your friend where you've been. We're in this together.'

She nodded.

He drove her back and watched as she walked up the steps to Chris's apartment, then sped off back to Cambridge.

That night, she slept better than she had for over a week.

10

Mulligans is one of those typically Irish bars only Boston or New York seem able to reproduce — oak and mahogany walls giving way at chest height to heavy mirrors with a small shelf between them to hold the glasses of Guinness, or Bud, or Miller Genuine, or any other of the ten beers the bar carries. The central bar area is crowded with the usual bottles of Scotch, Jack Daniel's, rye, bourbon, Canadian Club and Tanqueray, but also with Jameson's ten and twelve year old, Paddy, Powers, and Bushmills, Cork Dry Gin, Irish Mist and other genuine Irish products, their varieties of warm colour scintillating in the soft lights and reflecting in the mirrors. Black-trousered, white-aproned bartenders with their classic Irish features and deep brogues circle the bar area, dispensing liquid comfort, advice and solace, surrounded by the warmth of the animated conversation of those who appreciate a little bit of Ireland in the New World.

Mulligans Bar at 4 p.m. on a Tuesday afternoon bears no resemblance to the same bar at 6 p.m. on a Friday evening, when you can hardly move for the crush of bodies, hardly hear yourself speak above the noise of the crowd. Without the expertise of the bartenders, you'd hardly even be able to get a drink. It's not like that at all at 4 p.m. on a Tuesday. That's when Mulligans is quiet. The stools around the central bar are mostly empty; the booths around the edges are unfilled, but for an occasional couple, anxious not to be seen together for whatever reason, or a journalist, or academic, escaping from the world to do some writing in privacy.

Joe Kennedy liked Mulligans at 4 p.m. on a Tuesday. It was a time when he could break the day, wind down, cool off, collect his thoughts, see life from a different perspective. Maybe even have a quiet chat with Patrick Mulligan, the owner. This particular day, he looked like he didn't want to have a chat with anyone, as he sat at the bar, staring into his cup of black coffee.

Patrick Mulligan knew the signs. He was washing and drying the glasses which had accumulated from lunchtime, as he walked his patch behind the bar, also enjoying a break from the usual frenetic activity. One look at him would tell anyone with Irish connections that this was a man of true Gaelic stock. Probably a farmer. From the west. Galway, or Mayo, maybe Kerry. In fact, as Joe Kennedy knew, from long conversations on quiet Tuesdays, Pat hailed from Mayo and had indeed been a farmer until his eighteenth birthday when, after taking the cattle the seven-mile walk to the Ballymurphy market with his father and brother, had gone for a well-earned pint of porter in Houlihans. His brother, five years his senior, would inherit the farm when their father passed away — which wouldn't be long if he kept up the sixty Afton, and the bottle a day, as well as the usual pints of porter. And as he sat there in that small country bar and looked around, 18-year-old Patrick saw no other young men like himself. Maybe a couple his brother's age, and a great many older ones. He suddenly realized that if he stayed here, even if it was home, he would grow old owning nothing, doing nothing, being nothing. Just grow old. That was when, like so many before him, he decided to leave his native land, and take a little bit of Ireland over the ocean to America.

Just as Joe Kennedy's father had. They had a lot in common, Joe and Pat. Which was why Pat knew the signs.

'You OK, Joe?' he asked.

Kennedy looked up at the farmer turned barman and smiled. He could never be described as a handsome man, although occasionally, usually after a drink or two, friends had mentioned that he had a hint of Paul Newman about him. He assumed they were kidding. Sure, he was about five eleven, 170 pounds, short hair, thinning slightly, attempting not to go grey, blue eyes, and a friendly, lopsided grin. But that was where the similarity ended. I mean, Paul Newman is good-looking. And he doesn't have a small scar over the right eye, one under the left eye, and one under the right side of the mouth, which was *why* the grin was lop-sided.

'Sure, just too busy, as usual.'

But Joe was not happy. South Boston Homicide Division was busy enough without some madman rampaging through the state breaking black guys' necks and occasionally raping their white partners into the bargain just for good measure. And now, Senator Kingston. Shit! That was a crime against humanity, not just a random homicide. On top of this, it looked like the hit-and-run on Forest Road where the mother of Baby Jane Doe, the other big talking point of Boston these days, had died, was not a hit-and-run, but a homicide also.

Fuck! How come Joe Kennedy should get dumped with two of the highest profile cases for a decade, already attracting the attention of Fox, CNN, and all the other national news networks?

Did Joe Kennedy want to be famous? No way!

Joe Kennedy was your ordinary, run-of-the-mill detective, originally appointed to vice, which he enjoyed fine, before he made such a good job of that that he was promoted — promoted? — to homicide, where he had made such a good job of that that he was appointed Chief of Detectives.

All he really wanted to do was spend some leisure time. Visit Disneyworld with his girlfriend, Lisa. He was seriously thinking of just that, Disneyworld, when the county sheriff called to tell him that, after studying the tyre marks on the road, he believed that Jane Doe and the biker who was thought to be giving her a ride were probably the victims of a deliberate killing. That the marks on the road from what were Firestone tyres suggested that the biker had been run over twice, just to make certain.

And that made it homicide. Within the city limits. Joe Kennedy's business.

Shit!

He drained his cup and left the bar thinking he should have had a shot of Jameson's rather than a cup of black coffee.

Simone watched the Headline News too. She now knew that baby Jane Doe was Jenny's baby. Her baby. Still alive in the hospital. And she wanted her baby back.

The next day she drove to UHSM. Taking a deep breath she walked up to the reception area of the Premature Baby Unit. The evening receptionist looked up at her.

'Yes?'

'My name is Josie Stapleton. The Jane Doe who was brought in yesterday was my sister, Jenny. I've just come from Admin. They have all the details. They sent me down here.'

The receptionist eyed her up and down with suspicion. She'd already seen off three reporters that morning. 'Do you have any ID?'

Simone flashed her the fake ID, and showed her a picture taken some months before of her and a heavily pregnant Jenny together. The photo did the trick.

'Oh, I'm so sorry. What a tragedy for you. Does the father know yet?'

'The father's long gone. I'm hoping the authorities might allow me to bring up my sister's child. There's a lot of sorting out to do.'

'Do you want to see her?'

'I sure do. Just for a moment. Now she's born.' Her eyes filled with tears. It wasn't difficult. She really did want to see the child. When she'd heard on the news that the baby was alive she could hardly believe it. She'd remembered the impact, Jenny going up in the air, and the final sight of her lying by the roadside. How could the baby possibly have survived that?

'Just let me check with the nurse in charge.'

The receptionist left, returning just a moment later with a nurse who beckoned Simone through, taking her down a corridor off which were cubicles containing cots hitched up to piped oxygen, monitoring equipment and all the paraphernalia of high dependency care. They stopped at cubicle 7. The name on the door read Baby Jane Doe under which someone had pencilled in 'Orphan Annie'. She peered through the glass window. The baby was asleep. She had an IV but was not on a ventilator. There was only one monitor working.

'She doesn't need the hi-tech any more?'

'No,' replied the nurse. 'She's doing real well. She'll probably be on the normal ward in two or three days.'

After a few minutes, Simone thanked the nurse and turned to leave, glancing at the long corridor and the fire exit at its far end.

'Thank you,' she said warmly. 'I'm sure I'll see you again, and thanks for all you're doing for the baby.'

'You're welcome. I hope you get your wish to adopt her. Good luck.'

Thanks again, thought Simone as she left, but luck doesn't come into it.

11

Joe Kennedy was making his way along the corridors of the University Hospital of Southern Massachusetts to the Premature Baby Unit at UHSM to speak with Dr Reader when a familiar voice rang out, 'Who let that cop in here?'

He stopped in his tracks without turning and grinned the lop-sided grin. 'That wouldn't be Dr Anne Bell, would it?'

'Pretty good, Kennedy. Your years in the detection business haven't been totally wasted!'

He turned to see a smiling girl in a white coat. He shook her hand. 'Hi, Doc Bell. How are you?'

'Good, Joe. And you?'

'No problems, unless you care to include the Boston killer on the loose, the death of Baby Jane Doe's mother, and the countless other problems sitting in my in-tray.'

'Baby Jane Doe's mother? Was that a deliberate killing? I thought it was an auto wreck.'

Joe would not normally have discussed case details, but he had already worked with Anne

Bell on at least two cases, and had come to respect her.

'It's a real possibility. I have to check it out. I was just on the way to see Dr Reader and get some background on the baby.'

'I'll walk you over,' said Anne. They walked on, chatting like the friends they had become, Joe recalling their first few heated meetings.

Anne Bell did not look like the director of one of the biggest ICUs of all the university hospitals on the eastern seaboard. A diminutive but attractive 35-year-old brunette with serious blue eyes, the initial impression was one of a quiet, thoughtful, introverted academic.

Believe it at your peril.

Anne Bell was one of the most feared medical personalities in the UHSM campus. She was acknowledged as excellent at her job. She was also known as someone who hated inefficiency, would not tolerate sloppy medical practice, and was an unforgiving critic of carelessness and neglect. If surgical practice landed a patient unexpectedly on her unit, she would delve mercilessly into the details of the case to see if there was an avoidable reason. If there was not, she would fight tooth and nail to save that patient, and treat the consulting surgeon with respect and consideration. If there was an avoidable reason, she would fight tooth and nail to save that patient, and leave the consulting surgeon in no doubt that she knew why things had gone wrong and he had better be damn sure it never happened again. And if that surgeon tried to duck his responsibilities and give her a hard time, he would do so only once.

Anne Bell could out-shout, out-curse, out-think and out-wit any man in the hospital.

She had made it to the top against competition of the best of both sexes, and she knew as much about intensive care as anyone. But she had come up the medical ladder the hard way, and when you have to fight tooth and nail, against all odds, for something you value and want, then you protect it when you get it. Especially against inferior predators. She was perceived as single, ambitious, worka-holic, dedicated and professional. Beneath that image, unseen by her peers, she was also sensitive, caring, and vulnerable. Joe often thought what a great cop she would make.

They reached paediatrics and split, Anne going to a nearby ward and Joe walking to Dr Reader's office where he told his secretary he was expected. He was shown straight in.

John Reader was like many of the other hospital specialists Joe had met. In his fifties, neat grey hair, a tanned pleasant face, wearing a black jacket, grey trousers and black shoes with a white button-down shirt and sober maroon tie. It was their uniform whether they knew it or not, he thought. Joe sat down and got straight to the point.

'Thanks for seeing me, Doc,' he said. 'So the baby's OK?'

'Yes. She's fine. A little premature but getting over all the little hitches. She needs a couple of consults from other specialists before we can think of releasing her to the authorities; she'll be here for at least another week I should think. Possibly longer. But she'll be ready for the main ward in a day or so.'

'And the mother?'

'She was virtually DOA — dead on arrival. The team did an amazing job keeping her clinically alive until the baby could be delivered.'

'Sounds like it. Anyone come forward associated with the mother?'

'Not that I've heard. Admin would deal with that stuff. We'd probably be the last to find out.'

Bureaucracy, thought Joe, the same everywhere.

'Well, the medical examiner will want to get involved now. It's possible that the death of the mother was not an accident. That's something I have to look into.'

'You mean she was murdered? My God. Why?'

'Like I said, it's not certain yet. I'll let you know when I know.'

'Is Baby Doe in any danger?'

'I can't see why she should be. It was the mother who was murdered, and whoever did it clearly didn't give a f — er . . . fig about the baby. I suppose it wouldn't do any harm to put on a little extra security.'

'We've done that already to keep the Press away.'

'Good. Well that's all for now. Here's my card. Please send any details about the baby's discharge to me when the time comes, or anything else you think might help me. I'll get back to you if there are any developments you should know about.'

He stood and shook hands, leaving the paediatrician wondering who would want to mow down a 20-year-old mother on a deserted road at 5 a.m. in the morning.

Joe was wondering the same thing as he decided his next move should be to take a ride over to the scene of the accident and see if there was anything that might shed a little more light on the mystery of baby Jane Doe and her dead mother.

The Boston South Bank clock showed 12.22 a.m. as Peter Mendova sat in his car outside a fire-exit door on the road running past the UHSM Paediatric Hospital. In spite of the temperature outside, he was perspiring. Every now and then he would bang the wheel of the car, then look around furtively as if someone might hear him and come to investigate what he was doing parked there in the middle of the night. He had already seen one police patrol car in the distance but it was speeding to another part of the city. He wished he had been able to talk Simone out of this crackpot plan, but she was adamant. She looked on that baby as her property, which had been stolen from her, and which she had a perfect right to retrieve. She had told him to drop her off at 11 p.m. and be back outside the door at midnight sharp. Now he was wondering what the hell was going on, and what he should do if she did not show up soon.

★ ★ ★

When she left Peter, Simone, dressed in a spotless-white nurse's uniform, had caught the elevator up to the seventh floor. The nursing outfitters had assured her this was the type used by agency nurses used as extra cover at the hospital. She had hidden in a washroom for some time so as not to have to go through the night-time security access procedures then ventured out and spent the time walking purposefully around the hospital to make sure she would pass for legitimate. No one had stopped her or taken a closer look at the ID badge she was wearing. Now she took a deep breath and walked into the Premature Unit, past the unmanned reception desk, and down the corridor she had visited earlier that evening before the night shift came on duty. She could see nurses working in at least three of the cubicles, but not in cubicle 7. She walked confidently towards the door when a nurse came out of cubicle 6 almost colliding with her.

'Sorry,' she said, looking at Simone. 'You lost?'

'No,' Simone replied, glancing at her name badge. 'I've been sent up from the ICU to give a message to Nurse Pearce; she's needed down there for an hour and I'm to relieve her.'

'I'm Pearce,' said the nurse, clearly exasperated by the message. 'Shit, why can't they get their rosters right down there. This is the third time this month I've been moved around. What do they want this time?'

Simone shrugged, wishing she would just go.

'Don't know. I'm agency, but I'm fully trained, that's why they sent me.'

'I'll just call, see what they want,' the nurse said, walking towards the office.

'Please yourself, but they said it was urgent.'

Nurse Pearce grunted and decided to skip the call, go anyway, handing the things she was carrying to Simone with a curt 'You sort this lot out then.'

Simone breathed a sigh of relief. As soon as she left, she went straight to cubicle 7, switched down the volume on the monitoring equipment, bent over the cot, ripped off the adhesive electrodes on the baby's chest and scooped her up into her arms. As she exited the cubicle, she saw another nurse walking up the corridor towards her.

'What are you doing, Nurse?'

Simone didn't pause to answer. She started running towards the fire exit at the end of the corridor.

'Hey, stop!'

Simone kicked the door open and, taking the steps two at a time, dashed down through the fifth floor, the fourth floor . . .

She heard the heavy door she had come

through open and hoped the nurse had decided to give chase rather than alert security. She heard the footsteps behind her as she reached the third floor. Panting now, she continued on, past the second floor, suddenly hearing the door she had just passed on the third floor bang open. Now heavier, fresh footsteps were pursuing her, faster, closer.

She reached the ground floor and exited into the street.

The car was nowhere to be seen.

'No!' she screamed, waiting desperately for the exit door to open, praying that it wouldn't. She stood back against the wall, then saw the car appear and race towards her, the passenger door swinging open. Just at that moment, the fire-exit door crashed open. Simone stuck her leg out and the pursuing overweight security man fell over heavily, rolling on the sidewalk, grunting in pain. Simone leapt into the car hugging the baby to her, and screamed 'Drive!', then louder, 'DRIVE!'

Peter did as he was told and the Lexus screeched around the corner and away, only slowing two blocks later.

'Did he make the plates?' she asked, taking off the red wig.

'I muddied them out. Anyway, he was still

rolling when we took the corner. Shit, Simone, you did it.'

'Sure I did,' she gasped, 'but where the fuck were you?'

'A patrol car was beginning to take an interest in me so I had to go round the block. I didn't realize you were going to have half the staff of the hospital in hot pursuit!'

He grinned at her and she burst out laughing, stroking the crying baby's head before reaching into the bag on the floor for a bottle of milk. She shook it, and the baby took it enthusiastically. 'We only just did it though, Pete. I think our way of getting babies is easier than stealing them.' She gave a small laugh of agitated triumph. She was still panting with the exertion and the adrenaline.

'Shit!' she said, 'I did do it, didn't I?'

'Is she OK?'

'Yes, of course she is. I'll sort everything out when we get back. Look at her feeding. She's fine.'

Thirty minutes later, they parked the Lexus and took the baby to the nursery where Leanne was waiting to take over. Simone turned to Peter.

'You go to bed,' she said. 'I'll just stay here for a while and check her over.'

He nodded. 'Sure you're OK?'

121

She smiled. '''Course I am. I'm on a high. Couldn't sleep anyway.' Her eyes were still gleaming.

'Well, come to bed before the high wears off!'

'I'll do just that, Peter,' she said. 'I'll do just that.'

12

Joe Kennedy had driven around the city outskirts for a couple of hours after inspecting the crash scene with the local sheriff. It was a quiet area where the city merged into the non-specific land between Boston and Providence Rhode Island. Why would a pregnant young girl be out walking towards the city with no luggage at 5 a.m.? And who would be out driving over her and the biker who stopped to give her a ride? Door-to-door enquiries had not given the local police any leads and they were almost going back to the original theory of a hit-and-run. But the skid marks on the road suggested strongly that whatever vehicle had hit them had stopped then accelerated back over the crash site. He decided to go back to the office, check the biker ID again, check the local residents roster within a ten mile radius of the incident, and see where that might lead. He had just turned for home when his car phone rang.

'Kennedy.'

'Detective, this is John Reader here from the baby unit at UHSM.'

'Hello, Doc. Got some news for me?'

'Unfortunately I have. And very bad news. Baby Jane Doe was abducted from the hospital last night.'

'What?' Joe almost yelled the word into the phone, braking suddenly and putting the shift to park.

'I said — '

'I heard you. When? Who? Are the local cops there?'

There was a pause. Joe sensed that John Reader was in a state of semi-shock and wasn't enjoying the call much.

'When? At about twelve-thirty. A nurse and a security guard gave chase but couldn't catch the nurse who took him. That's the who. A nurse, or someone impersonating one. We have a good description, and the local police are here; they're checking the hospital security cameras now.'

'Thank you, Dr Reader. Sorry if I yelled. I was just so surprised.'

'That's OK, Detective. We're all in a state of shock down here. I thought you should know as soon as possible.'

'Sure. I'll come in. Oh, one more thing — was baby Jane Doe targeted, or could this just be an indiscriminate baby stealer?'

'This is a high security area, Detective; there are easier places to steal babies. And one of the nurses believes she recognized the woman who was heading straight for cubicle seven. There were other babies closer to the entrance and the fire exit she escaped through, which might have been easier to abduct.'

'Thank you for calling, Doc,' Joe said, replacing the phone.

So it was deliberate. No doubt about it now. This was double Murder One. And when the perp discovered the baby was alive, they decided to take it. But why? Why take such a huge risk of being caught? What made that baby so special? But it was simple now: find the kidnapper, find the killer.

'Oh shit!' he said out loud.

Kidnapping was a federal offence. He already had three Feds in his face over the killing of the senator. Now they might stick around even longer. Or bring more monkeys in to help. He groaned out loud and pulled the gear into drive. He should get back to the hospital as soon as possible and check this whole thing out before the trail went cold.

★ ★ ★

Sam Brown was consulting in the UHSM Physicians Building. The five-storey building contained suites of dedicated specialist

125

offices, waiting areas and examination-rooms where day-to-day out-patient consultations took place. He was due to see four new ante-natal cases and four follow-ups. He enjoyed these sessions. Getting to know the new patients before they started out on the journey together, and seeing the proud new mothers after delivery — this was what OBGYN was all about. These sessions also differed from the slightly chaotic public clinics at UHSM where he and his team might deal with fifty to sixty cases in the same time. But the private sessions brought in good money for the hospital as well as giving him well-paid job satisfaction. The afternoon drifted on until Sam's last follow-up case was shown in.

'Eleanor, how good to see you.'

Eleanor McBride was a tall, elegant lady of forty-five. She moved with the confident air of one who has no real worries in the world, least of all financial ones. The smart matching coat and hat and the ample jewellery underlined the point. She was holding a small baby in her arms.

'Hello, Sam.' She sat down.

'And how is Patrick doing?'

'He's quite splendid. Thanks to you.'

'You and Bill did all the hard work, Eleanor. I just supervised the process. May I?'

She handed the baby over to him and he walked to the examination couch. She followed him, wanting to stay involved, part of her refusing to let the baby out of her sight after all the trouble, and expense, it had taken to get him. Sam looked at the baby then checked him over looking at the face, eyes, ears, throat, chest and abdomen. He paused when he listened to the heart, listening to the *thub-dupp . . . thub dupp* of the heart sounds, but noticing something more. *Thub dupp-whoosh . . . thub-dupp-whoosh*. He put the stethescope away and completed the examination, checking baby Patrick's hands before allowing his mother to change the diaper as he washed his hands.

When they were seated, he looked through the notes again, finding what he was looking for and looking up at Eleanor.

'Did the paediatrician speak with you, Eleanor?'

'Yes. He told me Patrick has a minor heart defect. He gave it a name but I can't remember what it was.'

'Holt-Oram syndrome?'

'That's it.'

'So you know he will need cardiological supervision, and might need surgery at some point?'

'But reasonably straightforward surgery, I was told?'

'That's correct. Well that's OK. So long as you know. I didn't want you to be alarmed.'

Eleanor McBride was not alarmed. She had been, when the paediatrician first told her. They all thought William, her husband, was Patrick's father. Only three people knew he was not: herself, William and Dr Peter Mendova, whom they had paid $15,000 for the course of artificial insemination. The joy of the ultimate success had been intense. After years of fruitless investigations and tests, this doctor had delivered the goods. It had been worth every penny. She had asked him about the risks of birth deformities from artificial insemination and he had assured her that there was no greater risk compared with normal. He had confirmed the pregnancy, then suggested she continue with a local gynaecologist in the normal way. His role was now over. When she had heard that the baby might have a heart problem, she felt a slight pang of guilt and wondered if she should tell the paediatrician about Dr Mendova. Now she felt the same thing sitting opposite Sam Brown. But once more she decided against it. She wanted the whole world to believe this was Bill's baby. She even wanted Bill to try to believe it. The fewer people who knew their secret the better. And anyway, what difference would it make?

The baby's examination completed, Sam called in the nurse to take Patrick while he examined Eleanor. That completed, he smiled at her.

'Well, that's it, Eleanor. I'm here if you need me, but you won't need any more routine appointments. Your paediatrician will organize the cardiology appointment. It's been great meeting you and Patrick and taking care of things.'

She shook his hand.

'Thank you for everything, Sam. We'll never forget you. And if I get lucky again, you'll be the one I'll come to.'

They parted company and Sam sat down, thinking hard, going over Eleanor McBride's records. 'Holt-Oram syndrome.' He said the words out loud.

Two cases in one week. That was weird. He had never seen a case since med school, and now two. But everyone in medicine knew that things often came in clusters. There was a hospital superstition that everything came in threes. Well, one more case of H-O and Sam would believe it. He made a mental note to call into the library and look up the condition, check the genetics, see if it was more common in older primips like Eleanor. Also to check the hospital audit computer and see how many cases they had had in the past five years. He wondered what was happening at UHSM. Two H-O cases and one of them, baby Jane Doe, abducted from the hospital.

Too much to blame on El Niño.

* * *

The next morning Peter Mendova sat at the breakfast-table with his wife drinking strong black coffee. It was a crisp sunny December morning but the bright weather did not reflect his mood.

'Hell, Simone, it's all over the *Globe*. They even have a picture of you on the security camera.'

'Oh, grow up, Peter. Look at that photo, then look at me. That wig, that make-up. And anyway it's a crap photo. That won't get them anywhere. And they don't even have a description or make of the car.'

'But they're saying that Jenny was murdered: you told me it was an auto wreck.'

'It was,' she said. 'I crashed right into them. No choice. She'd never have come back. If she had she'd have tried it again. She'd have shopped us, Pete, one way or another. She

130

had to be silenced.' She shrugged. 'Shame about the biker.'

Peter looked at her in disbelief. 'Simone, you murdered them? You never told me that. My God, what's happening here? What if there were witnesses?'

'There weren't, and I didn't tell you because I didn't want to upset you. Peter, I had no choice.'

'Christ, Simone, you killed two people.'

'I'm a survivor, Pete. It was them or us. I love you.'

'What if the police start checking four by fours?'

'Let them. They'll find nothing on ours. The bull bar's been replaced. The rest of it has been scrubbed clean. Just a few dents now, like you'd find on any working Jeep.'

'Tyre marks?'

She slammed her mug on to the breakfast counter. 'I've changed the tyres. All four of them. Oh come on, Peter, how far are you going to take this? It will die down. Babies get snatched every week. People get killed on the roads every week. There's a mass murderer, a senator killer, out there to keep the police busy. We need to move on. We need another girl to take Jenny's place.'

'We could always move the entire operation to Chicago, Florida, the West Coast.'

Peter was still running scared.

'I don't want to move. What about the girls? The costs of setting up? We're on our way to our first million here, Pete, the first of many. In a couple of years we'll be able to retire. That's when we move to Florida. Maybe do a bit down there without the girls — your spunk stays up to scratch!' She smiled and gave his hand a squeeze.

'Stop worrying. Jenny's baby is home, and Lorene's is due in a month. You need to find buyers, so get your ass to work and let me do the worrying.'

He relaxed a little. Simone was right. As usual. He looked out at the frosty Boston morning; Florida in a couple of years sounded good.

'You're right,' he said.

'Trust me, I'm a doctor.'

'Oh yeah!' He got up, kissed her and left.

Two hours later, Elizabeth Davidson was shown into his office.

'Hello, Elizabeth,' he greeted her. 'How's Keith?'

She shook his hand and slumped into the chair. 'He's fine. I'm not.'

'Oh?'

She leaned forward, looking at him intensely. 'It's been three tries now, Doctor, and nothing's happened. I've just got a

132

feeling about this. A negative feeling.'

He felt the same. He returned her gaze. Christ, she was beautiful. He almost felt like suggesting that they forget the syringe and do the insemination the good old traditional way. Maybe that would do the trick. It would for him, that was for sure. He felt the beginnings of an erection at the thought and shifted slightly in his chair.

'What are you getting at, Elizabeth?' he asked, wondering if she was thinking the same as him.

'If I stop the AI now, how long would it take your Sisters of Compassion or whatever they're called, to get a baby?'

He wondered if this was the right time, with the papers full of the Baby Jane Doe affair, but he decided to press on. Business was business, and it was clear that this woman trusted him completely.

'Elizabeth, you couldn't have come at a better time. There's a sweet little sixteen-year-old child called Jenny in the convent who has just delivered. Everything seems normal. The father was a white, high-school kid. Excellent background. I delivered her myself. Once the baby is checked over, and I'm happy that the child is well, a two-week-old baby will be ready for adoption. As it happens, I don't have anyone else waiting at the moment.'

'Oh Peter . . . I never thought . . . so soon?'

A vision of her crying 'Oh Peter' in other circumstances flitted through his mind as she leaned forward, giving him a grandstand view of her 36Cs.

'Do we know the sex?'

He looked up at her face again. 'Would it make a difference?'

'No.'

'What would you prefer?'

'I'd prefer a girl, but Keith wants a boy. You know, keep the line going and all that. If we have to settle for one only, I guess a boy would be fine.'

'Do you want to know?'

She paused for a moment, then said, 'Yes.'

'It's a girl.'

She gasped and sat back. He could tell her brain was already working through names.

'Shall I draw up the papers, Elizabeth?'

'Oh do, Peter, do. I'll call Keith. There won't be a problem. So we're looking at maybe two weeks?'

'Yes. And remember, it has to remain anonymous. As far as you are concerned, you got her through a religious adoption agency. Neither your family nor your friends need to know the details. You kept it a secret in case there were problems so as not to upset people.'

134

She nodded. 'I know, I remember all that. God, Peter, you do wonderful work. I'm so grateful.'

How grateful? he wondered.

She stood up and he followed her to the office door. They paused and she turned to him. 'I'll make an appointment to call in with Keith next week to sign the papers and finalize the finances. Thank you again.'

And so saying, she reached up and kissed him on the cheek, just short of his mouth. He gave her a small hug and she left.

He turned and leaned against the door waiting for the erection to subside. Don't be greedy, Peter, he thought to himself. You can't fuck them all. Just your little girls at home occasionally when Simone's not around. That hypnoval was wonderful stuff. Zonked them out in seconds and produced retrograde amnesia. But that Elizabeth . . . she was something else. He returned to the desk thinking life was hard sometimes. And might get harder if he had to come up with another girl. But Simone was right. They were on a roll now. Jenny's baby was for the Davidsons, they had Lorene's baby to find a buyer for, but then there were no more pregnancies in sight. So a fresh girl was needed. And a decision if either Leanne or Lorene should provide a second, or if they should all be

135

ditched, dumped back on the streets where he had picked them up with no memory of where they had been or why. He sat down at the desk feeling a complete lack of control over his own destiny.

13

Sam Brown enjoyed fund-raising dinners, especially at the Rheinhart, where the food was always excellent. He had given a good speech, as usual, and had just sat down to tumultuous applause from the Rotarians. He reached for his glass of Cabernet. The talk was over; now he could relax. At first he paid little attention to the waitress with the serious face approaching the top table, portable phone in hand, until she whispered into the chairman's ear, and looked over at Sam in response to the chairman's reply, before walking towards him with the phone in her outstretched hand.

'Breech!' the midwife said down the phone, concern in her voice. 'Arrested labour; footling presenting; the resident can't get the baby out. Mother's bleeding. Early foetal distress.' She paused for a moment. 'Sam, we need help here. Sorry . . . '

'Set up for a section. Tell the resident to start without me if necessary. And don't let her *push*!' He would normally have asked who was on call and why they hadn't got *him* on his night on, instead of Sam on his night off. But it was Cindy on the other end of the line, and if Cindy called, it meant something was really wrong.

He made his apologies to the host and left, the applause breaking out again as the word went round that the doctor had to go to save another life. Maybe two lives. Might even be good for the fund-raising, Sam thought to himself wryly as he left. Should've thought of it before! God, that Cabernet tasted good . . .

It took him fifteen minutes to get from the Rheinhart ballroom to the delivery suite. He ran up the stairs, hearing the commotion from twenty yards down the corridor and, without even changing into his OR greens, he burst through the doors, surveying the scene, the noise stopping for a moment as all eyes turned towards the newcomer.

The patient was in lithotomy position on the table, wide eyes staring up from a face as black as his own, sweat on her brow; beside her sat a nurse, calming her, trying to calm her. Between her legs sat Nick Bailey, concern all over his face as he looked at a situation he'd never imagined even in his worst nightmares. They sure didn't teach you this one in the training programme. What was it with Boston? Beside him stood Cindy, green eyes staring at him above the mask.

Ready.

Projecting from the patient's vagina was the baby. At least, the baby from the neck down, tiny legs and arms moving, but only just, covered in birth juices and blood, head still inside, with a metal obstetrical forceps protruding alongside him.

'Christ!' said Sam, throwing his jacket on to the floor and crossing the room. 'Talk to me, Nick!'

The resident leapt out of his way.

'She just walked in off the street in advanced labour. Deep transverse arrest, baby not progressing. I put the forceps on to rotate him into a vertex, but she was panicking, pushing, wouldn't relax, wouldn't do what we said — '

'OK, OK, go on.'

He was in Nick's place now, feeling the forceps, feeling the baby's heartbeat, taking in the scene.

The scream made him jump.

'*Pleeeease* . . . you gotta save my baby, save him, *ayyeeee*.'

Her pelvis arched as another contraction racked her, the baby swinging grotesquely from side to side with the movement.

'You gotta do something *now*, or we'll lose it,' said the neonatologist.

Christ, thought Sam, tell me something I don't know!

'Ayyeeeee!'

The noise pierced him to the core.

'The foot appeared just before we called,' Nick shouted above the scream. 'We prepped for a Caesar then both legs came down, then the pelvis ... she just kept on pushing, pushing ... ' His voice died away as he saw Sam reaching on to the sterile tray for the scalpel. Not scrubbed, without hesitating, just reaching for the scalpel.

He wondered what he was going to do ... he knew it might take drastic steps now to save the mother, might even need to sacrifice the baby, but ...

The patient continued to scream and fidget until Sam spoke. 'Quiet, girl, just for a moment, while I get your son out for you.'

Suddenly there was silence in the room. It was like he had hypnotized her, her and the others, with his quiet, confident, voice.

'This will hurt, but just for a second. We don't have time for anaesthetics.'

'Just do it, Doctor ... ' The voice was calmer now.

He slit the skin above her vagina deepening the incision into the ligamentous membrane holding the public bones together in one smooth movement, and watched as the pubis widened. Just a half inch, but in some situations, half an inch is like infinity. She arched her back again as the knife went in, but this time not a sound came from her lips. The metal forceps fell to the tiled floor with a clang as he inserted his hand into the space given to him by the slight separation of the pubis, and deftly brought the baby out.

'Clamp!'

He didn't need to say it. Cindy already had it done, two clamps and a quick look at him for confirmation. He nodded.

She cut the cord and Sam leaned forward, putting the baby on his mother's chest, without letting go.

'Be proud, girl, he's beautiful, but we need to work on him now.'

Even as she reached for him a small cry split the air from the tiny blue body and Sam handed him over to the neonatologist.

'Do your stuff. Make him live. He'll never have it tougher.'

He turned back to Nick Bailey.

'OK, suture the pubic tissues back together, Nick, and put her in a pelvic splint, like they use for a fractured pelvis. Ortho-paedics will help you.'

He walked round to the mother, now lying motionless, totally exhausted.

'What's your name, ma'am?'

'Lily Greenaway, sir.'

'Well, Lily Greenaway, you've got a fine

young son there, but it was touch and go. You should've got here sooner, you know.'

'Couldn't, sir, I was alone, didn't know where to go, no one to help me . . . '

'Well, we'll look after you from here on in.'

He smiled and turned to go.

'Sir?'

He turned towards her.

'Thank you.'

He squeezed her hand, and she gripped his in return.

Nick was still standing beside him, rooted to the spot.

'What did you do?'

Sam walked over to scrub up and washed his hands and arms.

'Primitive stuff. Stuff I saw a long time ago. Never thought I'd need to use it. Called a symphysiotomy. Split the pubic symphysis to give yourself more room. They do it in the African bush for obstructed labour, when they can't do a section. Sometimes works.' He shrugged. 'She may have a few problems with gait, we'll have to see later. There was no choice. Remember it. You may never need to do it. But when you do . . . '

He turned to Cindy as the resident prepared to sew up.

'Thanks, you were right.'

She nodded.

'I'll go get some coffee, watch some TV in my office. The resident will call in on her later.' She nodded again preparing to help the resident.

He picked up his dinner jacket, pulled off the bow tie and undid the top two buttons of his shirt as he walked out of the delivery suite to his office. He threw the jacket on to a chair, fixed the coffee machine then sat down behind the desk, putting his feet up and flicking on the TV with the remote.

It was the closing stages of the Monday-night game. The Patriots were losing to Indianapolis 14-22.

The percolator spluttered its last gasp and he fixed a mug of coffee for himself. He was dozing when he became aware of the knocking.

'Yeah?' he grunted.

The door opened and Cindy walked in.

He jumped up and walked around the desk as she closed the door behind her. The kiss was long and passionate, no words spoken, none necessary. Eventually she broke away, looking up at him.

'Nice one, Sam. Told you we needed you.'

He smiled, as he walked to the coffee machine and poured her a cup.

'Just wanted to get me down here, Midwife James. I know . . . '

'True, but just for the patient this time. I never saw anything like that before.'

He handed her the cup. 'It's rare. But when it happens, there's not much time.'

They sat on the couch, close, talking, smiling, in the dim light. 'That your shift over?' he asked eventually.

She nodded.

'I'll check on the patient. Meet you out front. I'll walk you to the lot.'

'OK.'

He met her in the lobby fifteen minutes later. It was empty, except for the receptionist and the security guard. They walked through the glass doors into the cool Boston night.

'Winter's coming,' he said.

She looked behind her to make sure they were the only people around, before linking her arm through his. They walked slowly down the grass-verged entrance area, towards the dim parking-lot about a hundred yards to the left of the hospital entrance. There couldn't have been more than thirty cars dotted around the huge area.

'Where are you?'

'Over there, near the perimeter fence.'

They walked on, not in a hurry, wanting the walk to last. When they reached the car, she reached into her purse, took out the keys and flicked the central locking release. The lights flashed on and the siren gave a squeal.

★   ★   ★

He'd sat outside the Rheinhart, eating a Whoppa and listening to the game, settling down for a long wait, keeping the front entrance in view, ready for when the affair broke up. He sat up with a start when Sam Brown appeared unexpectedly at the front door and jumped into a cab at least an hour before he expected him to.

Alone.

He followed the cab to the hospital and parked in the lot nearest the entrance where he could see the comings and goings. He wasn't expecting this, had it all arranged for the other venue. He felt himself getting angry, so he took a snort to settle him, and switched the game back on. The New England Patriots lost 17–22.

He knew they would. There was work to do. He'd been called, and he was prepared. But now it seemed his plans were going wrong.

The guy must have been called into a case.

But suddenly he couldn't believe his luck, because when the black gynaecologist re-appeared at the front door an hour and a half later, he was accompanied by a girl. A *white* girl. Who was now linking arms like she was his girl, as they walked together towards the parking-lot.

He slid down in his seat so they wouldn't see him, but they only had eyes for each other anyway. He eased the car door open. There were just enough cars to give him cover, so that he could keep reasonably close to them. As soon as the cover ran out, he crouched, ready to run, run so fast that he would be on them before they knew it.

★ ★ ★

She opened the door and got in, putting the keys in the ignition and looking up at Sam as she reached for the belt.

She heard him before she saw him, Sam's body blocking the view. At the same moment, Sam heard him too as the sound of the soft sneakers on the tarmac approached, faster and faster, louder and louder. He half turned, but it was too late.

The big man hit him like a train, ramming him against the car.

Sam fell against the bonnet, winded, his back arched and the back of his head hitting the metal. Cindy screamed, but the impact had pushed the door shut, and no sound came. He spun Sam round, putting his arms under his from behind him, his hands meeting behind his neck, ready to snap it.

But Sam was no pushover; he was a big man and he fought back, his elbows working on the ribs, his foot stamping down the front of his assailant's leg, his body shaking from side to side, trying to work free.

But the other man kept his grip, trying to get his hands together behind Sam's neck, to regain the break position.

The door opened and he was aware of the girl, yelling.

For an instant the hands met and he pushed them forward. A snap split the silent air, and Sam went down. Now for the girl.

She had got back into the car, but the door was still open. She was rummaging in the glove compartment. He moved towards her just as she turned — with the gun.

'Get away! Get away!' she yelled, cocking the hammer.

He paused for an instant, but he knew he couldn't take her before she fired. He turned and ran, weaving from side to side, as the shots rang out, some close, none hitting home.

Cindy knelt beside Sam, the gun discarded. She felt for his pulse. It was there. Thready, but there, but he was not breathing. She leaned down to get at his mouth to start artificial respiration without disturbing his neck.

After six, she grabbed the gun, pointed it in the air, and emptied the chamber, yelling for help, then went back to her task. As long as there was a pulse, she'd give him air. She would give this man anything, her life if necessary. She shook her hair back off her face, and the tears from her eyes, as she went on and on until she heard the sound of feet running towards her. Within minutes, the emergency room team was on the scene and she fell back against the front wheel of the car, exhausted, watching as they worked on him, remembering his work in the delivery suite that night, then remembering the crack as his neck broke.

★ ★ ★

Billy James half walked, half staggered through the door of Mulligans Bar.

'Gimme a bottle of Coors and a shot of Jack Daniel's,' he shouted at the barman.

He knocked back the shot of whiskey in one, half emptied the beer bottle and ordered another round, then sat on a bar stool, still shaking slightly. He could hardly believe what he had just seen.

He had decided this was the night for

Cindy to be taught a lesson, so he had gone to the hospital before the end of her shift and loitered around the perimeter of the parking-lot until he saw her come out of the front door.

With him.

'Well fuck me!' he had said out loud, as he watched them walk towards the lot. So she *was* with a doctor. Well he looked like a doctor, a big black guy wearing a black suit. His grip had tightened on the butt of the .38 in his pocket when he saw them link arms.

He took a swig of the beer and half the shot remembering what had happened next. He had just been about to make his move when, out of the blue, a big — and boy was he big — white guy thundered out of the bushes on the opposite side of the lot and ran like an express train directly at the couple. He hit the doctor then got him in some sort of neck lock and the two struggled until the doctor went down. Then he turned to Cindy who was already in the car, but she got to the gun first and scared him off.

So his intuition was right. You're still a good cop, Billy James. She was cheating on him; it was with a doctor, a black doctor, whom the Boston maniac had just sorted out for him. Shit! What was this? Klan? In Boston? He raised his shot glass in a toast.

'To the Boston Klan,' he said.

The barman looked round at him. 'You say something?'

'Just toasting absent friends.'

So the doctor was out of it. A big favour. Thank you, Klan. Only Cindy to teach a lesson to now. And he wouldn't need the .38 for that. His fists would be quite enough to teach that little Irish bitch a lesson she would never forget. No one messes with Billy James, least of all Mrs Billy fucking James.

He got up to leave. As he lurched out of the door, he collided with a tall man coming in. He was about to launch into a tirade of abuse about watching where you're going, but the look the guy gave him and the feel of tight shoulder muscle under his suit made him think the better of it.

'Sorry,' he mumbled, and wandered off into the night.

Joe Kennedy made for his usual corner seat at the bar. Within seconds, Pat Mulligan placed a Bud draught in front of him. Joe sat staring at it, thinking how all the shit seemed to be hitting the fan at the same time. He needed a little time to think it through. The juke box was playing Jimmy Nash. Joe recognized the sentiments — there certainly were more questions than answers.

His mobile phone broke into his thoughts.

'Kennedy.'

'Peters here. I know you're not on duty, Joe, but I thought you'd like to know this. I'm at UHSM. The maniac struck again but this time he failed. The victim's in ICU but he's alive; the girl had a gun — she's OK.'

Joe felt a twinge of elation.

'Who was the victim?'

'One of the doctors, a Sam Brown, OBGYN at UHSM. Neck injury, unconscious, on life support, but stable. The girl is Nurse Cindy James. She's in shock, being looked after here for the night, under sedation. She should be ready to give a statement in the morning.'

'So we don't know if she saw him close enough to identify him. But maybe it's a break at last. You got everything covered there for now?'

'Sure. No problem, Joe.'

'I'm bushed, but I'll be over first thing. Call me if anything important comes up overnight.'

He switched off the phone. Maybe, for the first time, his luck was changing. If the girl had seen him, if she could make an ID, on what Joe already had . . .

He finished his beer and left feeling just a little better than he had when he arrived.

14

Sam Brown knew he was dying. It seemed like his life was flashing through the darkness of his coma.

London, England.

He was enjoying an after-theatre dinner with his mother in their favourite restaurant, Savori's, on the Strand. As usual the restaurant was busy and the atmosphere excellent, diners chatting and enjoying their meals on one of London's most famous thoroughfares. They had finished their main course and were on to dessert — a fresh fruit platter and brandy courtesy of the owner, a disarmingly handsome man who took good care of all his diners, but always took special care of Sam and his mother.

Following Sam's father's death, Nicole became unsettled in Washington and yearned to return to Europe. Washington was no place for a soldier's widow bringing up a son alone, and she felt the need to separate herself from the place of his tragic, unnecessary death. Any doubts about abandoning his final resting-place were tempered by her return to the city where they had first met. Before leaving she had secured a post at the American Embassy in Paris. After several years there she was offered a place in the London embassy. She accepted it and Sam completed his education in England before entering medical school at St Bartholomew's Hospital. He was as happy now as he had ever been. His mother was close by so he could take care of her. She enjoyed working in London, and they visited Paris often. The medical curriculum was demanding but he was handling it. Life was good.

Until that evening.

She broke into his thoughts. 'Sam, I have to go into hospital tomorrow for some tests.'

She made it sound trivial.

'What sort of tests? What hospital?'

'Yours, strangely enough. I've been feeling tired recently and the doctor ran a few investigations. It seems my kidneys are not quite up to scratch, so they want to do some further studies and maybe a biopsy.'

'A biopsy? Mom, this is serious. Why didn't you tell me?' He put his hand across the table and she held it for a moment, smiling at his concern.

'It's all happened quite quickly. The doctor got the blood results, made the calls, and tomorrow I go in. He said there's nothing serious to worry about, but they need to clarify a few things before advising treatment. He said it would probably just be pills, diet, that sort of thing.'

'Have you been given a diagnosis? A name?'

'No, I guess that's what this admission is all about.'

'Did they tell you the results? Mention a blood urea? Or creatinine?'

'Sam, I don't have a clue about those things. They've got it sorted. Don't worry.'

Sam looked at her. She was so beautiful, but perhaps she did look a little tired, pale. Why had he not noticed? He was a medical student after all. He should have noticed if something was wrong with the person he loved most in the entire world, the person he had been charged to take care of all those years before.

It's just you and your mom now, you take good care of her. How well he remembered the soldier's words.

'What time have you got to be there? What ward are you going into? Who's the consultant?'

She laughed. 'Sam, so many questions. I would have told you sooner but I knew you'd worry and I don't want that. Your studies are so important, I won't let anything interfere with them. I have a taxi booked, at seven. I go to the nephrology ward, D15, and the consultant is a Professor Millar.'

Sam banged the table.

'I know him — I spent six weeks on his unit. That's OK; I'll go and see him and tell him you're my mom and he's got to take special care of you.'

'Dear Sam,' she said, reaching for his hand again. 'He knows; I told him already. He actually said what a good student you were.'

She sighed and, for a brief moment, a look of sadness crossed her face.

'Your father would have been so proud of you. A doctor. I wish he could have been here to see you graduate. But I'll be there for both of us.'

She smiled and let his hand go, then raised her brandy glass.

'To *Doctor* Sam Brown.'

He smiled back, touching her glass with his own and they sipped the brandy, paid for the meal, and went home.

Three days later he answered his pager and was told to report to Professor Millar's office in Nephrology. He had visited his mother several times a day, and sat with her for as long as they allowed him to. The biopsy had been a little painful, but she had tolerated it with her usual resilience. The pager surprised him and he almost ran along the corridor to

155

the consultant's office, pausing to straighten his tie and fasten his white coat before knocking at the door. 'Come in.'

Professor Simon Millar was a tall, thin, studious-looking man in his fifties. His hair was greying and his face was pale. His eyes were a watery blue. He looked very tired. He stood up when Sam entered.

'Hello, Mr Brown, thank you for coming.' He pointed to the chair and sat down in his own, a serious look on his face.

'It's about my mother, isn't it?' Sam said.

He nodded. 'Not good news I'm afraid. The tests have shown that your mother has only one kidney. One in eight hundred people only have one kidney and in most it is of no serious relevance. Unfortunately, the biopsy of her solitary kidney shows evidence of leukaemic infiltration. Your mother has chronic lymphatic leukaemia in its terminal stages; I'm afraid there is nothing we can do.'

Sam sat, stunned, unable to move, unable to think. Professor Millar sat in silence, waiting for the news to sink in.

'There must be something, dialysis, a transplant? She can have one of my kidneys . . . '

Sam's voice rose with emotion as he realized the enormity of what he had just been told.

'Mr Brown, it's not just the kidney, although that will probably be the cause of her death, it's the underlying aggressive leukaemia which closes all the options.'

'How long?' he whispered, feeling unreal, as if someone else had asked the question.

'Weeks rather than months.'

Sam's eyes were suddenly full of tears. He blinked causing them to run down his cheeks.

'Does she know?'

'I spoke with her an hour ago. She asked me to explain the medical details to you, and let you know that she was going directly home. I'm desperately sorry, young man.'

Sam nodded, brushing away the tears and standing up.

'Thank you,' he said. 'I'll go to her now.'

He turned and left. Within an hour he let himself into his mother's apartment in Marylebone. She was waiting in the living-room. She stood up to face him as he walked towards her, and they hugged, a long, silent, painful hug before he said, 'There must be something they can do. We'll get a second opinion, go to the States if necessary.'

'Sam, I went through all that with Professor Millar. He saw me with another doctor, a haematologist. He told me the same thing. Apparently some leukaemias are so sudden and severe that there is literally nothing medicine has to offer. These are the best doctors in London, Sam, you know that. It's just hopeless and I have to face up to it.'

She paused for a moment, then said, 'Sam, I want you to do something for me.' She held his hand and they sat on the sofa together.

'If I am to die, I want to die in Paris. Would you take me there and be with me? I have already arranged to be buried in St-Germain-des-Prés, near where I met your father. There is a will; you are the only beneficiary, so the Paris apartment, this apartment and every-thing else will go to you. And I must ask you to make me a promise.'

'Of course, anything.' Sam felt like his heart was breaking.

'You must promise me that after I have gone, you will complete your medical studies. You must not drop out over this; it will make everything easier for me if I know you will become a doctor.'

'Of course, Mother, I promise.'

She managed a small smile. 'Thank you.'

Three days later they were in Paris. Sam had organized compassionate leave from his studies and they flew to Orly where a taxi was waiting. When they got to the apartment in Montparnasse, Nicole was tired from the journey and went to rest, leaving Sam alone. He was finding the ordeal worse than even he had expected. It had all been so sudden. How could it have happened? Would it have been curable if he had noticed earlier that his mother was becoming pale and tired? There must be something someone could do?

But there was not. The day after their arrival, Nicole took him to the Rue de Rivoli and showed him where the US forces had driven in to liberate Paris, showed him the exact spot where she had met his father. Then they had some lunch in the Café des Trois Magots at St-Germaindes-Prés and she showed him again where they had met when Richard returned to Paris. She had a wonderful time sharing her memories with Sam. That night when he brought up a drink for her and said goodnight, she kissed him and said, 'I had a wonderful time today, Sam. Thank you so much.'

She died that night in her sleep.

In the depths of his coma, a deep pang of agony racked Sam Brown's motionless body and he was aware of a tear slowly moving from his left eye and down his cheek. For a moment he thought he heard a voice calling his name, and he wondered what was happening to him.

15

'Where am I?'

The voice roused Simone who had been snoozing in a chair by the bed. She got up and stretched, then walked to the girl lying under the white starched sheets. She was a brunette with pretty eyes, presently ravaged by the drugs and street life she was leading, good, high cheekbones, and a slim body which would benefit from an extra ten pounds.

'You're in hospital. You were picked up off the streets near the common last night and brought here. You were dehydrated and suffering from an OD. That's why you've got the IV up.'

'I feel dizzy. Where's Jerry?'

'Who's Jerry? Your pimp? Your dealer? We know all about you, you know.'

'Fuck you. I want to get out of here.' She made to get up, suddenly realizing that her wrists were bound by restrainers. In any case, the movement made her so dizzy that she fell back on to the bed only semi conscious.

Simone smiled. She picked up the control button of the PCA machine and gave it two pushes. The machine injected another couple of boluses of methadone and diazepam into the girl's vein through the venflon intravenous set and within seconds she was snoring deeply.

She sat back on the chair, looking back at the door as it opened. Peter walked in quietly.

'How is she?'

'A little bit frisky, but she'll settle. We should be able to get rid of the IV tomorrow and get her moving with intermittent methadone and plenty of temazepam. She'll have to stay in solitary for a few more days, and I'll start the hypnosis as soon as she's ready for it, but by next week her memory should be wiped clean and she'll just assume she's always been here.'

'We'll have to watch this one. She's strong; she took a hell of a lot of force to get her into the car. Good job you're so slick with the IVs.'

'Well, we'll see how she goes. If there are problems we'll just dump her back in the city. Once the hypnotism kicks in with the drugs, she'll be just as submissive as the others.'

I hope so, Peter thought, because it's very tempting not to use a syringe on this one.

'How's Jenny's baby?'

'She's fine. When are you handing her over?'

'Next week. The blood tests should be back

161

by then and the Davidsons should have come up with the money. I'll call and fix it up for Tuesday.'

Simone took his hand suddenly. She led him out of the room and back to the kitchen where she sat him down, poured two cups of coffee, and faced him, a serious look on her face.

'What is it, Simone?' he asked.

'I've been thinking about what you said a few days ago. About it getting dangerous, going to Florida, remember?'

He nodded.

'Well, maybe you're right; maybe if we could make the money quicker, make a quick kill, we could close up sooner, then do it somewhere else.'

He nodded again, wondering what she was getting at. She was looking excited now, like she did when she thought of a new project, like she had when she kidnapped baby Jane Doe . . .

'I think we could up the ante, by providing embryo implants rather than just artificial insemination or the few live babies we can produce from these kids.'

He sighed, and she looked angry for a moment. She had heard those negative sighs before. She waited for the negative comment to follow.

162

'And where are we going to get frozen embryos from?' he asked, staring at the ceiling like an examiner before a poor student.

She smiled a little triumphant smile, and he knew she had all the answers already.

'From the University of Southern Massachusetts Fertility Centre, of course.'

He looked at her, knowing that his look was probably vacant, maybe even stupid, but this was too much for his ambitions to even contemplate.

'Explain?'

'When I did my unofficial stint there, looking for my little orphaned niece, I saw a sign to this lab, and I followed it. It is a little free-standing annexe outside the main hospital building. It was shut and locked up, of course, at that time of night, but completely unguarded. Peter, they would have dozens, hundreds of frozen embryos in their freezer, all labelled, all lying there, all waiting for months, years even, to be implanted into a willing and receptive uterus. Why should we charge two thousand five hundred for one AI session, when we can charge twenty thousand for an embryo implant? Hell, Peter, if we do twenty-five that's half a million on top of what we've got. Let's do twenty-five as quick as we can, then get out of here. You were

163

right. Let's go for the quick bucks, move down to Florida, and do it again there. Then San Diego. Then San Francisco. Peter, in three years we'd never have to think of work again.'

He looked at her, a long, passive stare stemming from his own sense of inadequacy and her incredible sense of ambition which bordered on the reckless.

'You're crazy,' he said eventually.

She looked hurt. 'Why?'

'It's a good plan, I have to admit, but how in the hell do you think you're going to get your hands on those embryos?'

'I'll steal them, dear Peter, dear Peter, dear Peter, I'll steal them, dear Peter.'

She mimicked the hole-in-the-bucket scenario perfectly.

'Like you stole the baby?'

'Exactly.'

'But it won't be as easy to get access to a locked lab as it was to walk on to the unlocked pediatric ICU,' he said, almost triumphantly.

'Why don't you let me worry about that?' she said, with a confident grin on her face.

He shrugged. 'It's a good plan, Simone, but you're upping the risk all the time. I don't want to lose you, and I don't want both of us banged up for twenty years. That was never the plan.'

'Peter, you're the one who's worrying. I think this is worth the risk. Let's go this route, and in six months we could be on our way to the sunshine state with at least half a million bucks in our pockets. Remember, Leanne has had her baby, Jenny is dead, and Lorene is about to deliver. Do we want Leanne and Lorene to get pregnant again? No time for that any more. And this new kid — I don't have good vibes about her, I don't know why. We may just have to get rid of them all. So the big bucks will be the embryos.' She looked at him, a long, confident, dominating look.

'Trust me,' she said.

He nodded, knowing he had no choice.

★ ★ ★

Anne Bell saw the tear run down Sam Brown's face as she sat beside him on the ICU and wondered what on earth was happening. It was Christmas Day. She had often been known to tell students and interns that there was no such thing as Christmas Day, Easter or Thanksgiving in the ICU. No such thing as day and night. Every minute was concerned with watching the patients, fine-tuning their metabolism and vital functions until they regained the ability to do it

165

themselves. Until they recovered enough to breathe and function independently of the tubes, lines, ventilators so that they could leave intensive care and return to their rooms, and home. Or until they died.

She had decided to lighten Sam up, try to wean him off the ventilator to see if he would breathe spontaneously and regain consciousness. It was her third attempt that week. The other two times there had been no response, and she was beginning to wonder if he would ever recover. So she tried again, left off the morning sedation, tuned the gases to try and stimulate some activity, to lighten him up, to make him breathe, to fight the tube sticking down his windpipe so they could remove it.

Which at precisely 3.20 p.m. is exactly what she did.

'C'mon, Sam,' she whispered at first, then louder, 'c'mon Sam, go for it!'

By 3.30 he was extubated and breathing through a T-piece on 30% oxygen. By 4 p.m., he didn't even need that.

Anne and the nurse talked to him the whole time, telling him what she was doing, where he was, checking his blood gases, his cardiogram, altering the IV, watching the frightened, confused eyes begin to brighten.

Occasionally she squeezed his hand for encouragement.

Before he squeezed hers.

She thought she'd imagined it, stopped what she was doing, looked down at her hand in his, then back at his face.

'Do that again, Sam,' she said.

He did. 'Oh Sam, that's wonderful.' Then, more seriously, she added, 'Now make my day and wiggle your toes.'

He did that too.

She bent over and hugged him, knowing he was going to be all right.

Maybe Christmas did happen sometimes on the ICU after all, she thought.

16

Peter Mendova was troubled. He was sitting at his office desk between patients, but his mind was only on Simone as he went over the increasingly reckless events of the past few weeks. OK, setting up the consultancy was great — safe, lucrative, and risk free. The only crime here was using his own semen in every case, but even if they were found out, the worst that could happen was losing his licence to practise in the state of Massachusetts. Big deal. Simone could carry on, or they could move out. The girls were something else, what Simone had called a 'logical extension' but that could be construed as kidnapping, and kidnapping is a federal offence. Then, murdering Jenny and some innocent biker. Murdering them. Then stealing the baby, and now thinking of going back to the hospital to steal embryos. And he was an accessory. No way he could lay the blame at her feet if they were caught. Oh no, they were in this together, hook, line and sinker. But what could he do about it? She was so strong, so committed, so determined, that he was simply no match for her. And if she got caught stealing the embryos, then all this other stuff would come out. What next? What would be Simone's next 'logical extension'? He sighed. For a transient moment, he wondered whether he should leave her, just get out, but he knew this was not an option. She scared the shit out of him at times, but they were a great team and he knew he had little choice. He was in this all the way, and the best he could hope for was that they got away with this embryo plan so that they could make a quick bundle, then disappear from Boston and start again somewhere. He sighed again and pressed the button for the next patient.

He stood up to welcome her, smiling as he watched her walk towards him. She was a tall woman in her early forties, with dark, Italian looks and a fashion sense that would put the Oscars' red carpet to shame. He was aware of her perfume and tried to hide his immediate reaction to her entrance, to appear professional.

They shook hands and he indicated the chair, before sitting at the opposite side of the desk and dividing his attention between her notes, and her movie-star looks.

'Mrs Polucci,' he started, 'I am Dr Peter Mendova. How may I help you?'

'Ah, Dr Mendova. Your name was given to

me by a friend Elizabeth Davidson?' She paused, checking if he recalled her.

He nodded, thinking that if he thought Elizabeth was attractive, this woman put her right in the shade.

'Good. I am one of seven girls. My sisters all have wonderful children whom I adore. I have none. I am the special aunt. The childless aunt. The only sister not to provide cousins. I spent five years and many thousands of dollars some time ago trying to conceive by every method known to medical science. It was a waste of time and money. My husband was very understanding. His sperm count was excellent. My ovaries were not. I gave up hope, until Elizabeth said I should just come and talk to you. She did not say why, or how you might help my ovaries, but she said I should come. So here I am.'

'I see. Did you try adoption?'

'Yes. The available children were all too old to enjoy as babies, or bond with from an early age. If they had offered me a child less than six months, we might have agreed.'

Peter smiled. It was all clear now. Elizabeth had decided that the Mendova ready-made baby service might be ideal for her friend. And she was right. He had been worrying for some time about the lack of women ready for Lorene's baby. The last thing they needed was

170

to keep a child in the house for weeks on end. The girls would get attached to it, and ultimate separation would be difficult, undermining the entire system. They had several AI cases in progress, but none was ready to proceed to adoption. Until now. He really owed Elizabeth Davidson one.

'Mrs Polucci, Elizabeth may or may not have told you that I have access to wonderful, newly born babies from a religious order who take care of potential unmarried mothers who reject abortion but cannot keep the children. From what you have told me, I think your chances of conceiving a child of your own are hopeless. But I may be able to help you.'

She leaned forward. 'How?'

'I have been told that a young girl is due to deliver within the next month. She cannot keep the baby — the family is Catholic and will not consider abortion. Their social status is such that they want to keep this entirely private, thus the involvement of the nuns and their nurses rather than their local hospital. Would you be interested in such a baby?'

It was instantly clear that she would. Her eyes brightened, her mouth opened a little, and she looked for a moment as if she was about to leap over the large desk and kiss him right on the lips.

As if.

'I would be very interested. Can I ask the characteristics of the parents?'

'I'm afraid the father is unknown. A local boy of course, but we have no details. The girl is dark-haired and brown-eyed. She could well be of Hispanic or Italian origin.'

'And you do all the tests to ensure that the child is healthy?'

'Everything is done by the book. We would not put up any child for adoption unless it was completely acceptable to the adoptive parents.'

Mrs Polucci leaned back in the chair and her eyes closed for a moment. She sighed, as if her wildest dreams were about to come true. When she spoke, it came as a whisper.

'I can't believe it. At last.'

He remained silent while the realization sank in, then said gently, 'Mrs Polucci, you said your husband *was* supportive. I presume he is still?'

She sat up slightly, disturbed from her reverie, suddenly frowning.

'I would like to say he is, but I would be lying. My husband died eight months ago, in an accident. When Elizabeth told me of you, I thought . . . a child . . . might be a little bit of him, even if it were not his own. I know if we had learned about you when he was alive, he would have come with me; he would have approved. I know he still would. I think Elizabeth knew also, which is why she told me of you. Will this make a difference? *Must* there be two parents for an adoption?'

He shook his head slowly. 'Not in your case, Mrs Polucci. So long as he has left you adequately provided for I will sign the appropriate forms after the formal counselling.'

She sat up, suddenly proud and independent.

'My husband was a very successful man, Doctor. Fifty thousand dollars will not be a problem.' As soon as she said it, her hand went up to her mouth.

Peter Mendova gave a small grin.

She had let it out. Elizabeth had told her about the possibility of a baby. The grin was accompanied by a momentary thought that if word of mouth got out of control, then maybe they should be thinking of leaving Boston sooner than they had planned. Loose tongues could mean trouble. But he was reasonably convinced that this woman and Elizabeth would not have been out blabbing. As far as he could tell, this was an arrangement between friends. For a moment, he felt slightly elated that he was going to help this beautiful woman fulfil a dream. Perhaps even felt the elation and satisfaction that doctors should feel in their job of curing, healing, of achieving the impossible for people desperate for help. A pang of guilt at his mercenary activities came and went.

'Well, that will be fine then, Mrs Polucci. Please come and see me in one week, and I will keep you up to date with progress. You can fill out the forms at that time, and I will need a down payment of ten thousand dollars.'

She rose from her seat and he walked around the desk to join her. She held out her hand.

'Thank you, Doctor. I cannot believe what has happened this morning.'

'I'm happy to be able to help you. I must emphasize, however, that this arrangement is strictly confidential. There are sensitivities about the mother, the order. Do you understand?'

'Of course. It will be strictly between the three of us.'

She knew he knew, and she gave a small smile of her own.

'The four of us,' she said quietly. 'Next week then.'

'Next week.'

He let go of her hand and watched her leave. The session had started badly, but it had certainly had a very satisfying ending.

Simone would be pleased. Might even give up the crackpot embryo idea.

★　★　★

Sam Brown was sitting out of bed within days of the assault. The neurosurgeons and neurologists had had a good look at him, and he had had two MR scans. It seemed that the crack that had split the night air when he was attacked was not the spinal canal snapping, in which case the spinal cord would have been severed and he would be paralysed: it was the left transverse process of the fourth cervical vertebra that had fractured, given him a temporary spinal shock, mimicking the more serious injury. The resulting onslaught to the vagus nerve had temporarily stopped his heart. He would have a sore neck, and might get pins and needles in his arms and legs for a few days, but he was told that recovery should be complete and he would probably be fit for office work in three weeks, surgery in six. Joe Kennedy had interviewed him a couple of times both with and without Cindy. He had not been able to help, but Cindy had given him a good description of his assailant and the entire incident. She was visiting him daily, realizing that the fact that they thought a lot of each other was probably the worst kept secret in the hospital and it was more important to see him than worry about gossip. He left the ICU on the third day, and was allowed home two days later. He was given instructions to take it easy, and wear the protective neck collar for the first week until the internal swelling and bruising settled. Anne Bell walked him to the front door of the hospital where Jerry Weinberg was waiting to drive him home.

'What can I say, Anne?' Sam said, turning to her before getting into the car.

'Now don't get all emotional, Sam Brown,' she said sternly. 'It doesn't suit your macho image, and anyway, if you start, I'll start too.'

He smiled. 'Well, how about just thanks, lady, and a hug?'

They embraced gently and he got into the car beside Jerry.

'And keep that neck collar on, Dr Brown,' Anne called after them, as the car pulled away for the short trip to Cambridge.

He followed instructions, took it easy, and kept the neck collar on. For two days.

By then, he was climbing the wall with boredom. He had tidied the apartment, got up to date with his paperwork, paid the bills, and watched more daytime television than was good for anyone. Cindy had called, and they had arranged dinner for the next day, which was Saturday. As he had his third cup of coffee in as many hours, he suddenly brightened. He was not confined to barracks. He could call a cab, go to the hospital, clear his paperwork there, then go to the library and swot up on that Holt-Oram syndrome.

Which is what he did.

He sat at the desk with Fitzpatrick's *Textbook of Cardiology* before him and read about something he had probably learned many years before, then had instantly forgotten in favour of more commonplace, everyday diseases.

This autosomal dominant condition was first elaborated in 1960.

So it was a genetic disorder, with a very high possibility of transmission from either parent to their offspring.

The cardinal manifestations are dysplasia of the upper limbs and atrial septal defect.

As he had found in Eleanor McBride's little Patrick, a heart murmur consistent with a small hole in the upper chambers of the heart, and a short thumb.

Arm deformities range from radial aplasia to hypoplasia of the clavicles and shoulders.

My God, thought Sam, not just the thumb, but absent shoulder bones.

Similarly, the atrial involvement ranges from none to major defects with considerable haemodynamic compromise.

He shut the book. So it could be a minor problem, or a very major one. And autosomal dominant meant that it was a definite familial, genetic predisposition. So, how many cases have we had here at UHSM in the past decade? The question was answered by a visit to the computer-room in the library. He logged in, and keyed Holt-Oram — 1992-2002. Within seconds the screen flashed the result. No cases.

He walked to the library office and picked up the phone, ringing pathology.

'Speak.'

The unmistakable, gruff Scottish tones of Jules Wellbeloved greeted him.

'Jules, it's Sam Brown.'

'Sam, how the hell are you? I thought when I heard the news you might be doing a guest appearance down here in the post-mortem room. You all right?' Jules was not known for his subtlety.

'Fine. Just a small query. Do you know the condition of Holt-Oram Syndrome?'

'Hmm, let me think. Is that the hole in the heart, atrium I think, and some sort of limb deformity? Rare condition. Why do you ask?'

'I'm impressed, Jules. I've seen two cases in the last month. I checked the UHSM records: they record none for the past decade. I just wondered if you see any at postmortem, but that they don't get on to the computer records.'

'Not seen one I can remember. The only reason I can recall it is because they had a bad one at the Brigham a few months back, and used it as a case for their clinico-pathological conference. I'd be interested in the details of your cases.'

'Well, one of them was the Jane Doe case that was in recently. You might check the PM details of the mother. She was DOA and would certainly have gone through the coroner's caseload. I'm going to speak to the mother of the other one to see if I can spot why he has it. I'll get back to you with those details later.'

'May just be a cluster, Sam. You know how it goes. I hadn't seen a hypernephroma for four months, and this week we had two.'

'I know. I've probably just got too much time on my hands. Thanks for your time.'

'My pleasure. Glad you're OK.'

Sam scratched his head, suddenly believing again in clusters. At the same moment he was aware that his neck was aching just a little, and he decided he had had enough. He called for a taxi and left for home.

17

Joe Kennedy had mixed feelings as he drove around the Massachusetts countryside in the area of the biker incident. One was elation, at the eventual outcome of the racial murders. The perpetrator was dead. An ex-pro-footballer called Greg Taylor had got into heavy drugs after the unexpected tragic death of his young pregnant wife in hospital. He had developed a fixation with the Klan, and started to target black men, particularly those with white partners on some sort of revenge kick. Police had eventually cornered him in a restaurant carpark. There had been a struggle, during which Taylor had got hold of a gun, but instead of turning it on the cops, he had given an anguished shriek of regret, as if realizing the enormity of his crimes, put the gun in his mouth and blown out his brains. He was a former friend of the New England Patriots quarterback Brad Ryan, who had filled the police in with the background.[1] He recalled that the doctor who had managed his wife's case was an Afro-American, and he thought this must have

---

[1] See *Serious Abuse* by Patrick Riley.

been the trigger to his confused, poisoned brain when he went off the rails. When the police searched his apartment, they found walls covered with Ku Klux Klan history and slogans, and newspaper clippings of the victims and coverage of their murders. He wondered if Sam Brown had been targeted because he was black, or because he was in OBGYN, sort of closing the loop. All in all, one tragic case.

Like this one. He had visited three farms and two mansions without any leads. The farm staff had been open and helpful. He didn't have a search warrant but his instinct told him that he probably didn't need one. The doors of the two mansions had been opened by maids who informed him that their masters and mistresses were out, and he should call later. They were both retired couples. He didn't think the call was necessary. There were four more houses to visit. Next on the list was White Plains.

It took about twenty minutes to get there. He stopped the car and got out to approach the intercom on the large wrought-iron gate. He pressed the button. There was no answer.

He pressed again, then again, but got the same response. He peered through the rails of the gate at the long dirt track up to the house. It almost looked unoccupied, but he saw fresh track marks on the drive. One looked like a saloon car, a big one from the width and separation of the tracks, the other probably a 4×4. He pulled out his mobile and dialled the sheriff s office and asked for the chief.

'I'm at a mansion called White Plains, Sheriff. It's locked up, very secure, and no one's home. Do you have any details on who lives here?'

The sheriff told him he would check and call him back.

Joe decided to finish the job. The next farm was like the others, and of the final two houses, one was for sale, and the snowbirds who had boarded up the other home were undoubtedly sunning themselves on St Pete Beach or some other piece of Florida paradise.

As he drove home, the phone rang.

'Joe Kennedy? It's Sheriff O'Malley here. White Plains is registered in the name of Dr Simone Belmont. She has a three-year lease. The realtor thinks she works in the city but doesn't know where. One year cash up front, not too many questions asked. Just glad of a buyer I guess; you know what realtors are like.'

'Did you check out this place in your initial enquiries?'

'We called three times but there was no

answer. It's still on the rosta to follow up.'

'Well I'll do that. Do you have a phone number?'

He did. Joe thanked him and drove on deep in thought. An MD, cash up front, with a 4×4. The only interesting individual of the day. He would call later and set up a visit.

★   ★   ★

Simone Belmont was sitting in the office of Dr Robert Feldman, one of UHSM's infertility experts. She had made a private appointment to discuss her infertility problem, and had just been shown into the office to meet the bespectacled dark-haired Jewish doctor. Robert Feldman was very proud of his unit. They had a good record of infertility treatment using all the most modern methods, and he had a good academic reputation for research and development, as he explained to Simone.

'We are waiting to move into a specially designed Assisted Conception Unit in the next month or two, so I apologize for the rather spartan surroundings you find yourself in, Mrs Barnett. Now, just go over your history for me one more time.'

'Well, I have had extensive pelvic inflammatory disease which has resulted in my

183

fallopian tubes being blocked. I had all the tests in Dallas from where I've relocated: laparoscopy, dye tests, you name it, I've been there. My husband has had testicular cancer, resulting in one testicle being removed, and radiation therapy afterwards. I don't have to explain to a doctor of your standing what that has done to his sperm-producing potential, though I'm just grateful to have him alive.'

Doctor Feldman nodded benignly. How he loved intelligent patients, especially those who knew their place and showed respect.

Simone was thinking how like Groucho Marx he looked.

'We've looked into it in a lot of detail. TESA and ICSI are out — he has no sperms to aspirate and I don't want anyone else's sperms to fertilize my egg and be injected back into me. I just don't want it.'

'So how may we help? I think I see where you are coming from, but I would prefer to hear it from you. I can see you're very knowledgeable about your problem. Do you surf the net?'

'Constantly. And when you've been through all I have, and been investigated at length by doctors like you at the top of your trade, you learn a lot.'

She shifted her position and took a deep breath. 'I believe this is one of the centres which has frozen embryos available for the treatment of infertility. Is that correct?'

'Yes, it is. We have a large store of embryos, some donated by mothers whose treatment has been successful, who have no further need of them, and some from paid volunteers. They are kept for research, where permission has been granted and ethical approval is forthcoming, and treatment for patients who are judged to be suitable cases.'

She sighed, as if in approval. 'And what constitutes suitability, Dr Feldman?'

'Failure of all other techniques, insuperable anatomical problems, and occasionally, in patients who make a choice and have the ability to pay an enhanced fee, since all monies received go directly into our research funds, and are an essential source of income.'

'Do I fit into any of these categories?'

He rubbed his chin, thoughtfully. She knew which category he would like her to belong to. He had an eye on business also.

'Well, with your double factor infertility . . . ' He paused, apologetically. 'What I mean is, you have both male and female factors at work here. Your husband is sterile, and you cannot conceive normally anyway. But you do, possibly, have healthy eggs in your ovaries, so a purist would say you ought to have artificial insemination by donor sperm using your own potential, rather than using up embryos which might be needed for people without that possibility.'

'I see.'

There was silence for a moment.

'And how much is a treatment cycle, Doctor?'

'Ten thousand dollars.'

Silence again.

'Are you a purist, Doctor?'

He smiled. 'Mrs Barnett, I am a realist. I would be prepared to compromise. I need to examine you, and obtain your records from Dallas. If what you say is correct, and I have no reason to doubt it, we might be able to offer you a cycle of two treatments.'

'Oh thank you,' she said warmly, 'that's wonderful.'

'Don't get too excited for now,' he cautioned. 'The success rate is still only twenty-five to thirty per cent. But that's better than nothing, isn't it? Now, shall we get the examination over?'

She had had worse experiences. He was very gentle and professional. When it was over, he asked her about Dallas.

'Oh, I have all the records and details at home; I'll drop them in in the next couple of days. Where do we go after that?'

'I will arrange some blood tests and a

pelvic scan. Once all that's completed, we can perhaps arrange a date.'

'That's fantastic,' she said.

'Good, well, I think that's everything for now,' he said, rising from the chair to see her out. She remained seated, looking up at him with big eyes.

'There is one more thing,' she said.

He sat down again. 'Yes?'

'Is there any chance I could just look at the embryos, get an idea of what . . . what they look like, what I am about to do with this body of mine?'

'Yes, of course. I can have a tech bring some across.'

'No, Doctor, I need to see where they are, what those little babies are doing while they wait to make someone like me so happy.'

Groucho Marx gave her a classic look. If he'd had a cigar in his hand, he would have tapped it with his index finger.

'You know, I see about ten patients per week like you. About a third of them ask to see what the embryos look like, but I think you are only the third person in five years who has made that request to visit them in the lab. But I know how important these sensibilities are. You are about to embark on a physical and philosophical journey, and if seeing the embryos helps, then why not?'

He stood up and escorted her out of the office, through the clinic area and into the open air. Twenty yards across a small grassy area was the run-down lab she had seen before.

'I told you we were coping in less than perfect conditions,' he said, apologetically. 'But when the new unit opens, it will be magnificent.'

They walked into the small whitewashed building. Half the area was taken up with flat waist-high refrigerators, with an aisle down the middle, almost like a supermarket. The other half was occupied by half-a-dozen technicians, working with test tubes, pipettes, and auto-analysers like any other pathology laboratory in the country. They barely glanced at her, and she kept her face averted. Doctor Feldman walked up to the third freezer on the left, pulled open the lid, and with almost a flourish of triumph, pulled out a stainless-steel rack.

Simone looked at it with fascination. The rack held about thirty long thin tubes, each around ten inches high with a tiny rubber bung at the top.

'Those are embryos?'

'They certainly are Mrs Barnett. Thirty wonderful, tiny little people waiting to happen. Aren't they magnificent?'

'But, how do you know who they are, where they came from?' Not that she really cared — for their purposes an embryo was an embryo, but she was fascinated.

'If you look along the side of each tube, and also beside where they sit, you will see a tiny bar code. That identifies each embryo. The computer carries the details of parents, physical characteristics, all that stuff.'

'And they are frozen? They can last . . . forever?'

'Well, indefinitely, we think.'

'What do they look like when they thaw out?'

'Small!' He gave a Groucho grin at his own joke. 'We have a special pipette' — he reached up to a wall-mounted rack above the fridge and brought down a surgical-looking syringe instrument — 'into which we suck the contents, then implant the embryo into the recipient womb through a hysteroscope.'

'I can't believe it's so simple. How wonderful. And such a shame it can't be more widely available.'

'I couldn't agree more.' Groucho was warming to her increasingly. 'But it's the same with, say, transplants. We could always use more hearts, livers, kidneys. The need is massive and the supply totally inadequate.'

He put the embryos back in the freezer and hung up the applicator.

'Well, are you reassured?'

'I certainly am, Dr Feldman. I want to thank you from the bottom of my heart. I will get the Dallas data back to you soonest. I'm really excited about this.'

'I'm so pleased. Let me show you out.'

Driving back to White Plains, Simone knew she was right about the embryo project. It was almost too good to be true. They were stored in a poky little laboratory behind the main hospital with just one door. But she might not even have to risk breaking in. What had Groucho said when she asked him if she could see the embryos?

I can have a tech bring some across.

Totally nonchalant. Just bring some across.

So if a nurse should turn up at the lab, and say *Dr Feldman sent me over to pick up some embryos to show a patient*, what would they do? Probably just hand them over. Worth a try? Less risky than a break-in. But then, why bother? Why not just inject sterile water into the patients, tell them it was an embryo?

She frowned. No, many of these patients were like the woman she had just portrayed — knowledgeable, well read, experienced in failures from previous futile attempts. They might ask to see the embryos, might know what they look like. And anyway, they would be vulnerable. Desperate. Why shouldn't we help them? Maybe Peter was right: let's do it properly, she thought. Let's get hold of the little things, charge a fat fee, and give the patients a chance. We might be bad, but we're not that bad.

18

Peter Mendova was humming along with *Warm 94 FM* as they drove to Copley Square. Today was the day they were handing over Jenny's baby to the Davidsons. Baby to them, $50,000 to him. Everybody happy.

He had given the receptionist the day off, and no further appointments had been arranged. They reached the building at 9.30 and carried the cradle up to the office. The baby was snoozing gently, the result of the bottle of warm milk laced with a little Phenergan that Simone had given her a half-hour before.

At 10 precisely, the office doorbell rang.

Elizabeth and Keith Davidson greeted Peter like an old friend, while Simone stood obediently by the cradle in her nurse's uniform.

Elizabeth bent over and looked at the child who was about to become her own, while Keith went with Peter to his desk to do the business.

'May I hold her?' she asked Simone.

'She's just fallen asleep — it might be as well to just take a peek and let her rest.'

Simone gently took off the blanket covering her and let Elizabeth inspect her, check that she really did have two arms and two legs.

'She's wearing a standard Pampers diaper, and has had a feed of Biobaby dried milk about an hour ago. The bottles have been sterilized using Milton. She has been feeding three to four hourly, her bowel movements are normal, and she slept for six hours last night without waking once. This bag contains what is left of bottles, Milton and all that, though I'm sure you've got your own?' She smiled and Elizabeth nodded.

'This envelope contains her basic neonatal observations and blood tests, all of which have been normal. She ought to have a further check-up in four weeks with a pediatrician, who will then probably hand her care over to your primary-care physician, but she is a happy, healthy little girl.'

'Thank you, Nurse, that's all very clear.'

Keith appeared at her side and peered into the cradle. 'Everything OK, Liz?'

'Everything's wonderful, Keith. Can you believe it? We've got a little girl.'

He smiled, sharing her excitement, and flashed a glance at Peter Mendova.

'Thanks seems inadequate, Doctor,' he said, 'but thanks anyway'.

'It's a happy day, Keith, Elizabeth. I think

Nurse here is going to miss your daughter, but that's what she is now, and good luck to you both. In fact, to the three of you.'

'Sure. Well, we'll be on our way then.' He shook hands with Peter, and picked up the cradle.

Elizabeth shook hands with Simone, then turned and gave Peter a warm hug of intense gratitude.

'Thank you, thank you so much,' she whispered.

'Sure,' he whispered back.

They left, and Peter gave Simone a hug.

'You know, what we're doing is not that bad, is it? Did you see them? They were ecstatic.'

'I agree. Some people might not, and we've bent the rules almost beyond a circle. But that was quite moving. So where do we go to celebrate?'

Yes, it was a good morning for Peter Mendova. But, unknown to him, that feel-good factor was not going to last all day.

★ ★ ★

Joe Kennedy was becoming exasperated with White Plains. He had called at least seven times, without success. Occasionally he got an answering machine, usually no answer at all. A further visit to the area had been just as unhelpful as the last, but the fresh 4×4 tyre marks told him that the house really was occupied. His gut instincts told him that either this was one real busy MD, or that it was somewhere maybe worth getting into. He decided that he would pay a late evening visit next time, and not go away empty handed, even if it meant a little inspection of the grounds without a search warrant. Sometimes rules had to be bent just a little.

★　★　★

By the time they reached home, Peter and Simone had had a slap-up lunch at the Copley Plaza, accompanied by two bottles of champagne, and were ready for a few more. They parked the Lexus in the yard and went into the house.

'I'll just check the girls,' said Simone. 'Why don't you open a bottle of Bollinger?'

'Good plan,' he replied. He had just got the foil off when he heard the scream, followed by Simone's yell from upstairs.

'Pete, come quickly!'

He took the stairs two at a time and rushed into the corridor leading to the rooms. Simone was with Lorene, Leanne standing behind her. Lorene was rolling about the bed in obvious agony.

'Shit. Is she in labour?'

The wet floor gave him the answer even before Simone responded.

'I don't think there's time to get her down to the delivery suite. She's fully dilated.'

'We'll deliver her here without the epidural. I'll get some Demerol.'

He returned a few moments later with a syringe, and leaned down to speak to the young girl.

'Lorene, listen, it's Peter. I'm going to give you an injection for the pain. Don't push unless Simone says so, you hear? Don't push, Lorene, till you're told.'

He slipped the needle into a vein in her arm and injected a hefty dose of Demerol. At the same moment Lorene screamed again, and Simone said, 'Here it comes. Hell, this kid must have done this before.'

The head appeared as Peter yelled at Lorene not to push, then a shoulder, then the chest and second shoulder, and in a jiffy it was out.

A bonny, bouncing boy.

Peter looked at the child in silence, his jaw dropping.

'Get the clamp, Peter, for the cord, then get some oxygen, quick!'

It was indeed a bonny bouncing baby, a bonny, bouncing *blue* baby. And it wasn't crying.

He handed the clamp to Simone then ran down the stairs to the delivery room for the oxygen. When he got back, Leanne was sponging Lorene down, and Simone was listening to the baby's heart.

'Christ, Pete, there's a huge murmur here. This kid's got a major cardiac problem.'

'And a rudimentary shoulder and thumb; Simone, look at this arm.'

He handed over the oxygen and she put the mask to the baby's face.

'Well,' he said, checking Lorene, 'what do we do now?'

Simeone was thinking hard. This was totally unexpected. And this baby looked sick enough to be terminal.

'We've got two choices, Peter.'

He looked over the baby at her. 'Yes?'

'We either take him to hospital . . . ' She paused for a moment, then continued, 'Or we let him die and bury him here.'

He stared at her, realizing what she was suggesting.

'What's this? Another *logical extension*, Simone? You've got to be joking.'

She glared at him. 'No, Peter. I'm serious.'

'But is it necessary? We've blown it here, ended up with a sick baby. It happens. No reason to let it die. Come on, Simone, we did take an oath back there when we qualified.'

'Oh, Mr Scruples all of a sudden. Where did this come from? We're in shit up to our eyeballs here, and you want to get Catholic on me?'

'Shit? Sure, most of it yours. I didn't drive over two people. I didn't suggest kidnapping these girls.'

'Oh no, Peter, that's because you haven't got the balls. You're behaving like a wimp, and that's not the man I married. For God's sake, get real.'

'So you want to bury the baby?'

'That would be the safest thing to do.'

'No!' He shouted the word.

She threw down the oxygen mask. 'Then sort it yourself,' she yelled, and stormed out of the room.

He watched her in disbelief, suddenly wishing he'd kept his mouth shut.

He looked at the baby. God, he thought, he does look sick. He suddenly felt angry. Right, Simone, I'll show you, he thought.

'Leanne,' he barked, and the youngster jumped. 'I'm going out. Look after Lorene. Give her sips to drink, and sponge her down now and then. If she bleeds from her vagina, call Simone on the intercom. Do you understand?'

She gave a slightly dazed nod, stroking the

groaning girl, still semi-conscious from the Demerol.

He wrapped the baby in blankets and put him in the cot they had prepared, then carried it down to the garage. He put him in the passenger seat of the Lexus, walked round to the driving seat and started the engine. He gave one look round, almost expecting Simone to be there to help, before pressing the accelerator and heading off in the direction of the University Hospital of Southern Massachusetts.

★ ★ ★

Back at White Plains, Simone was in the study sulking, furious at her husband's attitude. Shit, she thought, we're here to make money, not to weep over wasters. Things were going well until Peter started losing his nerve. That baby won't make it to UHSM, so let nature take its course. Some you win, some you lose. We lost. So when did Peter suddenly get a conscience? What is going on in this relationship? She suddenly felt she was approaching a cross-roads in her chosen life, and needed to consider which way to turn. Especially since she had missed her last two periods and started feeling nauseous first thing every morning. How she wanted to have Peter's baby. But it was not the right time. And it could be the same as the child she had just condemned to death.

For a rare moment, the ever capable, ever confident Simone Belmont felt a pang of uncertainty about the future. The intercom from upstairs interrupted her thoughts, and she wondered whether or not to answer it.

★　★　★

Peter drove as fast as was safe with the cot on the passenger seat, looking down every moment he could to make sure the baby was alive. It was a twenty-minute drive to UHSM and the roads were not busy. The baby gurgled and cried a little, and he began to think that they might make it in time. But what to do then? Take it into the ER? Dump it on the sidewalk and hope someone finds it? He was still undecided when he entered the hospital grounds so he drove up to the ER and past it to assess the situation. It was quiet. One ambulance unloading a case, one or two people standing around making mobile phone calls, or smoking. He had taken the licence plates off the car, and he decided to make another circuit, then simply dump the cot on the sidewalk outside ER.

He drove around the corner slowly so as

not to arouse interest, then parked and walked around to the passenger side. He took out the cradle, and placed it on the pavement outside the ER. A young girl, perhaps a secretary or clerk, peered into the cot with interest, then watched as Peter walked back to the car. When he got into the driver's seat, he wasted no time, hitting the accelerator and speeding off. He glanced at the rear-view mirror, seeing the girl run out to the edge of the pavement to watch, then turn to look at the baby. He knew she would alert someone, call a nurse from inside. The baby would be taken care of.

When he got back to White Plains, Simone was in the living-room, a whisky glass in her hand and an angry expression on her face. He helped himself to a glass of wine.

'Well?'

'I dumped him outside ER. He'll be looked after.'

'Great. Are you happy now?'

He didn't acknowledge the question. 'Lorene OK?'

'Yes. But I think this part of our work is coming to an end. I don't want to wait nine months for the new girl to deliver for fifty thousand when we can get more than that in half the time with the embryos. I'm going to get them tomorrow and we'll start. Then we'll move out.'

'Together?'

She gave him a long hard look without answering.

'Why the sudden urge to close up and move out?'

'Have you checked the answerphone recently?'

'No. Who calls us anyway?'

She stood up and walked to the sideboard, then pressed a button on the machine.

Hello, this is Detective Joe Kennedy of the South Boston Police Department. I need to talk to someone at White Plains. Please call me on my mobile, 07386 340392 as soon as possible.

'Holy shit!'

'It's probably just a house-to-house about Jenny. I'm surprised they've not been in touch sooner. But I think we might need to dump the girls, grab the embryos, do as much business as we can in the next few weeks, then get out of here.'

'Why not go now?'

'Because if I get those embryos and you find just ten patients in the next few weeks, that could be two hundred thousand dollars. Let's clean up and clear out. We can always move faster if the cop looks like trouble, but we've got to dump the girls in case he is on to us and gets a search warrant.'

Dump the girls, Peter thought. Just like that. But she was right. If some cop was thinking of snooping around, the last thing they needed was to have to explain why three drugged zombies were living with them. He felt a transient pang of regret. Leanne had almost been part of the project, and had borne a child of his. Jenny was dead, but her child was sold and Lorene was still recovering from her labour.

'OK. Let's do it your way. How do you want to let the girls go? All together, or one at a time?'

'I don't know. Let's think it through first. We have to decide where, when and how.'

'Maybe, like the baby, leave them outside different hospitals so they'll get taken care of?'

'You're all heart, Peter,' she said, with a hint of sarcasm.

'Look, Simone, I don't give a shit about the new girl, we can just dump her where we found her. Sooner the better in fact. You've already taken care of Jenny.' He paused for a moment to let his disapproval register. 'Leanne and Lorene are different. They've been our friends for the past year. No trouble from either of them. Gave us a hundred thousand dollars' worth of babies. They deserve a chance.'

She nodded. He was right. Leanne especially had been a companion, almost welcoming her escape from the streets to the refuge of White Plains, enjoying the pregnancy, but letting the baby go without a murmur. Perhaps these had been the best months of her life as one of the Mendova sect, with a roof over her head, a large apartment to live in, a garden to tend to, a kitchen to work in. She almost felt a pang of regret that Leanne would be deposited back in the city. Maybe she could stay on till the end. One girl in the house would not be a problem. Christ! she thought. I'm beginning to think like Pete again.

'Leanne's special,' she said eventually. 'Maybe we dump the new girl, leave Lorene outside a hospital with a few hundred bucks in her purse, and let Leanne stay for a while longer?'

He looked pleased. Now she was being reasonable. He had almost expected her to suggest they just bump them all off and bury them in the cellar. Maybe he was overreacting to her attitude.

Perhaps she had had no choice but to total Jenny and the biker. After all, this was Simone, the love of his life, the brain behind their project. Where would he be without her?

He moved towards her and put his arms round her waist. She looked slightly surprised.

'What's this? I thought you didn't approve of me any more.'

He kissed her on the cheek, then the chin, then the lips.

'You should know better, Simone. We're a team. Always were, always will be. Let's dump the new girl tonight. I'll call the cop tomorrow and arrange to see him at Copley. No point in him snooping around here. Seeing him there will give us an advantage over him, maybe put him off whatever trail he thinks he might be on.'

Simone looked a little doubtful, wondering if he could cut it. Maybe she should see the cop herself.

He sensed her doubts. 'Don't worry, Simone, it will be OK. Now, let's have that champagne, then get rid of little Miss Trouble upstairs.'

They dumped her later exactly where they had found her. There were no problems.

19

Sam Brown had only been back at work for thirty minutes when he got the call from John Reader.

'Sam, how are you?'

'Good, thank you. Nice to be back.'

He wondered what the call was for; the Chief of Paediatrics and Sam did not cross paths that often.

'Just thought you might be interested in an emergency admission a couple of days ago. Do you remember our chat about Holt-Oram syndrome?'

'I sure do. We got two in a very short time.'

'Well, make that three. A little boy was dumped outside the ER on Friday evening. Just dumped. A car sped up, a guy got out with a carry cot and put it on the ground, then got back in and drove off. No plates, patchy description, a patient waiting for her husband to pick her up saw it, and took the kid into the hospital. Bad case. No shoulder and a very short forearm. Major heart defect. Been to surgery, now in the Cardiac ICU. Doing OK.'

'Hell, John, we all know about clusters, but

this is weird. Do you have any ideas?'

'None. Did you check on how many cases we get here?'

'Sure did. None in ten years. Now three. OK if I drop in and look at the baby? This is like continuing medical education here.'

'Of course. And let me know if you get any ideas. There's at least a *New England Journal of Medicine* publication here.'

Sam smiled as he put down the phone. Those academics, always trying to get their name in lights. But funding often depended on output so he saw where Reader was coming from.

He leaned back in the chair and shut his eyes. Why, after ten years of no cases, should he have encountered three in as many months? What could be the explanation for it?

Baby Jane Doe, an infant plucked from her dead mother's womb, the victim of a hit-and-run or even a murder, Eleanor McBride's baby, and now, this little guy dumped on the street. Apart from Eleanor's child, two very unusual circumstances.

He flicked the keys on the computer-pad to bring up patient details, then found Eleanor McBride and called her number. It was some time before the phone was answered, but he recognized her voice immediately.

'Mrs McBride, this is Dr Brown. I'm sorry to disturb you. How's everything?'

'Fine thank you, Doctor. What can I do for you?'

'Well, I'd very much like to talk with you about the baby. We've had three cases in a row of that Holt-Oram syndrome we spoke about, and I just need to make some enquiries of the people involved.'

'What sort of enquiries?'

'Well, just a chat really.'

'I don't understand, Doctor. You have been wonderful with us. We have a lovely baby with a small problem. It's just one of those things. I don't really think I can help you in any way.'

'I just wanted to ask about the family histories of you and your husband, see if we can find any other clues as to why we should have a mini-epidemic.'

'Doctor, I greatly value your care of me and baby Patrick, but I don't think we can help you with this matter. Goodbye.'

The line went back to the ringing tone, and Sam sat staring at the hand-set. That was so unlike Eleanor McBride, he couldn't believe it. Why should she have been so insecure and uncooperative? He put down the phone and sat deep in thought for a few moments before leaving for his first appointments. He wondered if John Reader had reported the dumped baby to the police, and made a mental note to call Joe Kennedy later.

* * *

Joe Kennedy was walking into the impressive lobby of 1171 Revere Street looking for the offices of Dr Peter Mendova. The message on his voicemail had given him the details of where to locate the owners of White Plains during office hours, so he had called to make an appointment with the husband of the woman who had leased the house. The receptionist in the lobby confirmed his appointment and indicated the way to Suite 23A where, after a short wait, he was shown into Peter Mendova's office.

He walked towards the large desk, sizing up the smartly dressed doctor who had risen from the chair to greet him. They shook hands and Joe flashed his ID. Peter Mendova gave it a cursory glance, then said, 'Detective Kennedy, welcome. Please, sit down, and tell me what I can do for you.'

'Well, at the risk of getting off on the wrong foot, could you tell me why you took so long to return my calls?' He accompanied the question with his lop-sided grin to soften the enquiry. Beneath the grin, he really wanted to know.

'Oh, sorry about that. We've been out of town, and when we've been here, it's been hectic.'

Joe smiled and nodded, remembering the fresh 4×4 tracks at White Plains.

'So what can I do for you?' asked Peter.

Joe took out his notebook.

'Are you aware of the death of a pregnant young hitch-hiker and a biker some weeks ago?'

'Of course. Everybody knows about that. It was a terrible tragedy.'

'I'm checking all properties in the vicinity to see if anyone knew the girl. She was carrying no luggage at the time of her death, so her hike clearly originated somewhere in this area.'

Peter Mendova rubbed his chin. 'I see. Can't help you, I'm afraid.'

Joe looked around the office. 'You're a gynaecologist?'

'Yes.'

'And your wife?'

'She's an MD, currently not working. We've been doing up the property, so she's taken a sabbatical.'

'The dead girl wasn't a patient of yours, then?'

'No, I told you, we didn't know her.'

Joe was silent for a moment as he consulted

his notes. Then he fixed Peter with his most piercing blue-eyed stare before saying, 'Do you have a four by four automobile, Doctor?'

Peter was ready. 'Sure, everyone around here has a 4×4. The Jeep is my wife's. I usually drive a Lexus, but I'm in the Jeep today. It's in the parking-lot. Want to see it?'

Joe nodded. Were the doctor's answers just a little too confident, too immediate?

He followed him down the hall to the parking area at the back of the building where Peter indicated the Cherokee Jeep. Kennedy walked around it slowly. Did the bull bar look slightly newer than the rest of the bodywork? It was hard to tell, for the car was in good general condition.

'New tyres?' he asked.

'Relatively new. They wear out pretty quick you know.' Kennedy noted that they were Goodyear.

Not Firestone.

'Am I a suspect, Detective?' asked Peter.

Joe paused in his circuit and looked at him. 'Doctor, everyone within thirty miles of here is a suspect. It's a hell of a coincidence that she was pregnant and you're a gynaecologist. But that apart, you're no more guilty than anyone else. We have to check these things. No need to call a lawyer.' He smiled. *Yet,* he thought.

'Well, Doc, thanks for your time. We can leave it here. I may just need to run a few basic tests on the car — we're doing it to all the four by fours in the area. Nothing specific. Tyre treads, paintwork, you know. I'll give you proper authorization for it when I can get round to it. We're pretty busy at the moment.' He shrugged.

Peter Mendova smiled. 'No problem, Detective, any way I can cooperate, just let me know.' We've got it covered, he thought to himself, pleased with his morning's work, and the way he had handled the cop.

Joe shook hands with him and walked towards the exit.

He, too, was pleased with his morning's work. One coincidence you could accept: *a gynaecologist living in the area near to a pregnant woman's death.*

Two coincidences you might accept: *a possible new bull bar fitted to his Jeep.*

But could you accept three coincidences?

Four new tyres, not the usual Cherokee Firestones, but Goodyear.

The thought that perhaps three coincidences were one too many made him very interested in the doctor working out of 1171 Revere Street in the upmarket area of Copley Square. Very interested indeed.

20

Simone Belmont left White Plains early, leaving Peter sleeping. She was in her nurse's uniform once more but not wearing the wig and disguise she had used to snatch Baby Doe. Instead, her hair was slicked back under the cap and her make-up applied in such a way as to disguise subtly her true appearance, and make her look faintly oriental.

She had not woken Peter because she did not want any further confrontation about stealing the embryos. For God's sake, she thought, as she drove towards Boston, those embryos are not specific to any couple, they are surplus to requirements. They are just sitting there freezing. Why not offer them to some new customers? No one loses except Dr Groucho Feldman, and there were plenty more embryos in his fridge anyway. And we make a quick fortune and leave town richer than we ever expected, and set up somewhere else. She smiled to herself. You sound like you're trying to justify yourself to Peter, she thought. Might as well have woken him up! She shifted in her seat, thinking about the rows they had had over the previous few months. She loved Peter and they were, as he always pointed out, a team. But he was losing his nerve more often these days. She hadn't wanted to kill the biker but she had no choice. She was a survivor, and if that meant she had to do the surviving for both of them, so be it. He was just a typical, talented, weak male.

It was nearly 7 a.m. when she reached the hospital. Traffic on the campus was busy with day shifts arriving and night shifts leaving. She found a space at the edge of car-park 7 from where she could just see the small white building across the grass from the Out-Patients Building. Her research had confirmed that Dr Feldman would be consulting in that building from 9 a.m. She settled down to listen to the early morning radio. She would test the uniform shortly by going to the staff restaurant for a coffee.

By 9.10 she was ready. She took a deep breath and set off for the Out-Patient Building. She would have to approach the lab from that direction in case anyone was looking. It had to be as authentic but relaxed as possible if it were to work.

She reached the corridor on the ground floor where Dr Feldman had his office and walked towards the exit, then stopped abruptly in her tracks. For there, walking

214

towards her, briefcase in hand, was Groucho Marx himself. There was no choice, she had to bluff it out. Would he recognize her? Her heart racing, she walked confidently towards and past him.

'Good morning, Nurse,' she heard him say, suddenly realizing he was talking to her.

'Good morning, Doctor,' she replied, without breaking her stride, letting out a quiet sigh of relief as he walked on.

She managed a smile then before leaving the exit and heading towards the lab.

The adrenaline's flowing now, girl, she thought to herself, no point in delaying things.

The lab was as she remembered it — the small white-washed building, the flat, waist-high refrigerators, with the aisle down the middle, almost like a supermarket. The technicians were in place, working with their test tubes, pipettes, and auto-analysers.

She walked up to the third fridge on the left where Groucho had performed his magic and spoke to the nearest technician.

'Dr Feldman has asked me to bring over some embryos to show a patient.'

The young man didn't move, he just looked at her.

Oh God, she thought, what have I done wrong?

He looked at her name badge then back at her. 'He was only here a moment ago, he didn't say anything about this.'

That's why he was walking this way, she thought, then said, 'He just arrived in the office a moment ago. The first patient was waiting. She had already requested to see them this morning, but he had completely forgotten. He sent me straight over.'

'Oh, that's OK. He's not best known for his memory, is he?'

The technician winked, opened the fridge and handed over the stainless-steel container.

'Thanks,' she said, taking them carefully and turning for the door with a sense of relief.

'Oh, Nurse Lee-Ming.'

She paused and turned her head.

'You need to sign this for them.'

He put the docket on the fridge and she signed it H Lee-Ming.

'And remember, no more than five minutes, and bring them back personally.'

She smiled and made for the door.

'I'd like to see you again,' he called after her.

Small chance, buddy, she thought as she walked out of the building purposefully.

She carried the container to the ground-floor ladies toilet where she had hidden the small hold-all. She put the embryos into the hold-all, then made directly for car-park 7. There was no more excitement on the way. She deposited the embryos in the freeze box she had brought with her, took off the nurse's hat, and kicked the 4×4 into action. She felt elated, just as she had when she retrieved the baby. She had done it. They were in business.

* * *

Sam Brown was surprised to get the call from Eleanor McBride. He was in his office working through paperwork.

'I've been thinking about what you said, Dr Brown. I don't want to seem uncooperative with you. It's just that the matter is . . . sensitive . . . to say the least.'

'You can trust me, Eleanor. I just need to ask you some questions. It will be between the two of us.'

'Can I come over and see you?'

'Sure. I'll be here all morning. Just tell the receptionist that we have an appointment.'

An hour later they were sitting face to face in his office. She looked anxious.

'It's about this Holt-Oram syndrome, isn't it?'

He nodded. 'We've had none for ten years,

then suddenly we've got three. Your little fellow, and two very strange cases. Did you read about the Baby Jane Doe whose mother was killed on the freeway?'

'Of course, she has it too?'

'Yes, but there's more. A very severe case in a newly born infant who was left at the front of the hospital recently, just dumped, abandoned. So of the three cases, two are surrounded by very suspicious circumstances.'

'That's weird, kind of . . . horrible.'

'I just wanted to check on your family history, Eleanor. Ask you a few questions.'

'Go ahead.'

'Does anyone in your or your husband's family have any history of cardiac problems?'

'No, not to my knowledge.'

'Any deformities, however trivial, of the arm, hand, thumb?'

'No.'

'Any other physical problems, or family failings?'

'We have always been a horribly healthy lot, Sam.'

Her mind was racing. Should she tell him their little Patrick was the result of artificial insemination? That Bill's family history was totally irrelevant? And what of Dr Peter Mendova? Did he know these facts. Could these other cases have anything to do with him? She needed time to think.

Sam was continuing his questions.

'Sorry,' she said, 'I lost concentration for a moment.'

He smiled. 'I just asked if there had been anybody in your family who has suffered multiple miscarriages with no obvious explanation?'

She shook her head again.

'Has the paediatrician seen Patrick again yet?'

'No, he didn't seem to think there was any great urgency.'

Sam realized he was drawing a blank.

'One last request, Eleanor. Can we get a blood sample from Patrick and run some DNA tests? They will be completely confidential, and you will be kept fully informed of the results.'

Eleanor looked agitated for the first time. Sam noted that she seemed angry.

'What is this, Sam? Paternity tests on Bill? What on earth are you suggesting?' She stood up to leave.

'No, Eleanor, tests for the Holt-Oram gene to try to identify it and its characteristics.'

He didn't want to upset his patient, but it was obvious she was not to be placated.

'Sam, I'll have to give this conversation some measured thought, and talk to Bill about it. But no blood test. Understand? No blood test.'

With that, she walked quickly out of the office, once more leaving Sam puzzled and none the wiser.

21

Joe Kennedy liked endings, conclusions, closures. Not speculation, uncertainty, and unfinished business. The Boston Maniac case was closed. But the biker killing was still cold, apart from the fairly fragile theory that the OBGYN smoothie he had interviewed at Copley Square might be involved.

And that theory was fragile. Here was a respectable successful gynaecologist who worked in Copley and had a nice ranch in the country upon whom Joe was seizing as a suspect, primarily because he didn't have any other route to go. He gazed into the Boston sky from his office and wondered if he could get a search warrant for White Plains on the flimsy evidence he had so far.

Well, Your Honour, he might have a new bull bar, and his tyres are now Goodyear . . .

I don't think so.

The phone interrupted his thoughts.

'Detective Kennedy?'

'Yes, who is this?'

'Sam Brown, OBGYN at UHSM.'

More fucking gynaecologists Joe thought,

then regretted the implication. Sam Brown was an OK guy.

'Hi, Sam. You OK? Back at work?'

'Yeah, I'm fine now. Can I run something by you?'

'Sure. Want me to come over?'

'I'll come to you. I could do with getting away from here for a short time.'

'I'll be here.' He put the phone down.

At the hospital, Sam made for the car-park. He wanted to have a drive, put *Les Mis* on the CD player, get his thoughts together before he met with the detective. He turned the car out of the hospital and on to the highway for the short trip to the city centre. Twenty minutes later he entered the South Boston precinct and was shown to Detective Joe Kennedy's office.

Joe got up to meet him. Sam noticed how high and untidy his in-tray looked. The out-tray was empty.

'Well, Sam, glad to hear you're out of danger. How's it feel to be back at work?'

'It feels great, Detective. Never thought I'd miss it so much.'

Joe wondered whether to ask how Nurse James was, but remembered Anne Bell's comments as Cindy had sat, daily, by his bedside. Something about two very nice people with things to sort out.

Instead, he asked Sam what he could do for him.

Sam recounted the Holt-Oram scenario.

Joe leaned back in the swivel chair.

'So two of the three Holt-Oram cases occurred in highly suspicious circumstances,' he mused, feeling a knot of anticipation in his stomach as he thought of the lack of progress with the Jane Doe case. 'First, Jane Doe, whose mother died with a biker, a case we believe to be murder and, second, a baby dropped at the hospital.'

He fixed Sam Brown with a direct gaze.

'Doctor, there's something kind of weird happening in the world of Boston gynaecology.'

'Tell me about it.'

There was silence for a moment.

'Any theories, Dr Brown?'

'Well, the question is, given the weird circumstances, can we assume that somehow or other, one gynaecologist is involved with those two babies?'

'How could that be?'

'Only two ways. One, by a huge coincidence. What we call a cluster. It happens. You get no cases for years, then three come along at the same time. There used to be a joke about buses doing the same thing when I lived in London.'

'You lived in London? How was it?'

A transient image of his mother flitted through Sam's brain. 'Nice while it lasted,' he replied quietly.

'Or?' prompted Kennedy.

'Or one guy who carries the Holt-Oram gene supplying the semen for artical insemination of infertile women.'

Joe gave a quiet whistle. 'You've got to be joking, or as John would say, you cannot be serious!' He was quite unprepared for the concept.

'I know it sounds outrageous, but it's a possibility. An outside chance. I'd go with the cluster theory but for one thing.'

'What's that?'

'The third case.'

'What about it?'

'She's an older lady who tried for some years to conceive. She finally made it. When I interviewed her recently, I asked if I could DNA the baby to look into the H-O gene. She became very defensive and angry, asking if I was questioning the paternity of the child. I wasn't, but later I began to wonder if, perhaps, she had gone down the artificial insemination path and not told me about it. Somewhere in private practice.'

'She wouldn't say?'

'No.'

'So if she did, and she named the gynaecologist then we might start making real progress.'

'Possibly. But we can't force her.'

Joe thought for a moment. 'Sam, I need time to digest this. It's a murder case, and it is possible that a judge would demand her to admit it and name him.'

'Only if I named her first, Joe, and I'm not, at this moment, prepared to do that.'

Joe stared at him, incredulous. 'Sam, this is a murder case for Christ's sake. You must.'

'No, Joe, I must not. Not at this stage. She is my patient. These are theories. The coincidence option remains the most likely, with my patient telling the truth, and being totally innocent. Until she opens up to me, I cannot open up to you. There's too much for that family to lose.'

'Not if she's innocent.'

'Joe, whatever she's done, she's still innocent. She hasn't committed any crimes.'

'Not until she obstructs a murder inquiry.'

Sam stood up, suddenly angry. He was beginning to wish he had kept the matter to himself. 'Joe, I always rated you as a human guy, not an aggressive cop.'

Kennedy leaned back and sighed. 'Me, too. You took the words right out of my mouth.'

He liked Meatloaf. He also liked Sam.

'OK, Doc. Let's play it your way for a little while, and I'll pursue my own inquiries. But I have to tell you, there might come a time when I do have to get tough. And believe me, I don't want to hurt you or your patient.'

Sam prepared to go, offering his hand. 'I believe you. I'll keep in touch.'

Joe shook his hand warmly. 'Thanks for coming.'

He showed Sam out and returned to the desk. He took one look at the in-tray, then swivelled the chair in the opposite direction, leaning back and closing his eyes to ponder on what he had heard, an image of Dr Peter Mendova forming an impressive backdrop to his thoughts.

★　★　★

Billy James had been stalking Cindy for seven days, first finding where she was staying, then getting some idea of her shifts. It wasn't easy. Meant he had to stay sober to drive the Oldsmobile around without getting done for driving under the influence. Even so, he knew if he was pulled over even early in the morning, he would doubtless be positive. Most of the time his blood was 5% alcohol. He recalled it took one hour per unit to metabolize one shot of anything from the moment you had the last one. That usually meant he had around sixteen to eighteen shots to metabolize at around midnight. Given that he would start drinking within ten hours of the last shot anyway, he was always going to be seriously out of hours to spare. And that assumed a normal liver, which his probably was not.

He was past caring.

Since he saw his wife, *his wife*, leaving the hospital with the black doctor, he had been waiting for the right moment to teach her a lesson.

And this was it. The gun was in his hip pocket. He had had enough shots to feel good but not enough to be careless. Now he was waiting in the parking-lot near her car, waiting for her to walk over.

He was dying for a drink but he knew this was not the moment. He could go celebrate later, like he did when the black guy caught it from the maniac. Christ, that was a good moment. Well, tonight would be just as good.

He saw her coming. He felt the Viagra kick in. This was going to be good.

She reached the car and clicked open the

driver's door. Just as she got in, he opened the passenger door and jumped in beside her.

'Hi, bitch,' he said, pointing the gun at her head. 'We've got a date.' He cocked the .44 and said menacingly, 'Now drive.'

22

Sam Brown was in a deep dream when the phone rang.

He finally picked it up and grunted, 'Yeah.'

'Sam. It's Anne Bell here. From the ICU.'

He rubbed his eyes and glanced at the clock. It was 3.30 a.m.

'Anne, what is it? I don't have any patients — '

'Sam, it's Cindy. Just get here.'

The line went dead. Cindy? What was she talking about? Cindy? In ICU.

The memory of the bruises of the past came and went and he suddenly knew. He leapt out of bed and showered quickly. Slacks, shoes and a shirt were enough before he ran to the drive and jumped into the car to head for the hospital. The roads were deserted. It didn't take long.

The ICU was busy as usual, but he spotted Anne immediately and headed over to her.

'Sam, it's not pretty, I have to warn you. Some maniac has raped and beaten her half dead. It might be touch and go. She's young and strong, but she's lost a lot of blood and her kidney function seems deranged. I didn't know whether to call or not . . . it's none of my business . . . I just thought you should know.

'Thank you, Anne, I should know. Can I see her?'

'Yes, but be prepared.'

He was, but he still nearly collapsed when he saw her. Cindy was on the usual ICU life support systems, but even so he could see the bruises, the swelling. Her face was barely recognizable as a face, more a mess of bruised flesh with tubes sticking through it all. Her right arm was in a short-term splint. Fractured. The catheter bag from her bladder was draining blood rather than urine. The two IVs were running, one with saline, one with blood. She had a tachycardia, the pulse racing at 130. The monitor showed her blood pressure to be 90/60. He looked at Anne. She saw the anguish.

'Shit, Anne, we're losing her.'

'Steady, Sam, this is the best she's been. Believe me. She's coming up from the initial crisis. It's the next few hours that matter. We've got to get the CT scan, monitor the bloods, keep the CVP up, and exclude any further internal bleeding. Then we might have some idea. And some chance.'

'Who's the surgeon?'

'Morales.'

'That's OK. The urologist?'

'Jerry Weinberg. She's in good hands, Sam.'

He relaxed a little. 'Yes, with you too. My God, Anne, someone here tried to kill her. Where was she found?'

'Dumped on the west Common. About ten o'clock. The cops found her on routine patrol.'

He took a deep breath. 'Can I stay?'

She squeezed his arm. 'If you want. They'll be coming to take her to CT in a while. Stay till then; then go home. Come back when you get into work later. We should have a better idea then.'

'Will you still be here?' he asked.

She gave a resigned smile.

'I'll be here as long as this one takes, Sam.'

It was 6.45 when he got back to find Anne with Dr Morales and Jerry Weinberg in her office.

'Hello, Sam,' said Jerry, surprised to see him.

'Hi, Jerry, Peter.'

There was an awkward silence before Anne said quietly, 'Cindy has no one. She left her husband some time ago. Sam has been watching over her. He has a personal interest.'

Jerry patted him on the shoulder. 'Hell, Sam, I'm sorry. Real sorry.'

'Thanks, Jerry.' Sam knew he meant it.

'What's the score?'

'She's got extensive bruising, abrasions, vaginal tears. The uterus and bladder are intact. Peter here doesn't think there are any internal abdominal injuries at this point, but an exploratory laparotomy has not been excluded. The biggest problem here is that Cindy only has one kidney. She was clearly born that way.'

Jerry Weinberg paused for a moment, that moment when any doctor hates the words he has to utter next.

Sam recognized the moment. 'And that kidney is damaged?'

'Yes, Sam. It's ruptured, with some tearing of the calyces, the internal drainage systems. It's leaking internally. In normal circumstances we would consider removing it. But here . . . '

The explanation was not necessary.

One equals one.

Jerry continued, 'I'm asking Al Pollard, the uroradiologist, if he can get some nephrostomies in. If we can avoid major surgery at this stage but get tubes in to drain the kidney, divert the urine, give it a controlled route to stop internal leakage, then possibly, just possibly, the tears may heal. So long as the main tissue doesn't bleed from the rupture. The kidney filters a lot of blood. If that blood leaks internally, there will be no choice.'

'Emergency nephrectomy and dialysis. Or transplant?'

'Exactly.'

There was silence. Sam nodded. 'The bastard.'

They looked puzzled.

'What?' asked Anne.'

'Her husband. He did it.'

'How do you know?' asked Peter Morales.

'She had bruises for months while she was with him. He's a drunk ex-cop who beat her regularly. She moved out after a real bad one.'

He looked at them and shook his head.

'Sorry, just thinking aloud. May not be him at all. We'll have to leave it to the police department.'

Dr Morales gave a small cough. They all had work to do. Sam got the message.

'Thanks, guys, for everything. Please keep me posted. I'll get to work and call in later.'

He left them to their deliberations and headed for his office, his brain in turmoil. He asked his secretary to get him a cup of coffee and sat at his desk. It had to be the husband, Billy. Who else? He had seen the bruises, talked with her about him. There was no other suspect. He had to call Joe Kennedy.

But hang on. He had already called Joe Kennedy once, and the meeting had not been that constructive. Oh, he saw where the cop was coming from, but it was all theory. Like this case. Cindy could have been raped by anyone. Every major city had its share of rapists, perverts, waiting for their opportunity. Hell, how many times this year had he been called to ER to see young girls, and old ladies for that matter, mutilated by deranged, or drugged, or drunk men with no objective other than to satisfy their own primeval desires. Who says this was Billy?

He decided to think a little before talking to the cop. Suddenly he felt uneasy. Was this going to be a deal? Joe, you go get Billy James, and I'll give you Eleanor McBride's name? Or should he go after Billy James himself?

He called in to the ICU at lunchtime, but Cindy was in X-ray. He went back later to find that Al Pollard, UHSM's foremost uroradiologist, and a man of immense experience and technique, had indeed got three nephrostomy tubes into the upper and lower regions of the kidney's internal collecting systems. Urine was now coming out of all of them, rather than draining internally. He had also got a drain in the tissue around the kidney to let out the urine which had accumulated there already.

Good job, thought Sam.

At 6 p.m. he called in again. Anne Bell was back on duty. She looked disturbed.

'What is it?' he asked.

'Kidney function's going off.'

'But she's got the nephrostomies in.'

'They're slowing down. I think the kidney's going into ATN — acute tubular necrosis. Shock. The filters stop filtering. The poisons aren't excreted. They accumulate in the blood. Kidney failure, Sam, in its purest form.'

Sam clutched at the chair and sat down. He had been down this road before.

'Not good news I'm afraid. The tests have shown that your mother has only one kidney. One in eight hundred people only have one kidney and in most it is of no serious relevance. Unfortunately, the biopsy of her solitary kidney shows evidence of leukaemic infiltration. Your mother has chronic lymphatic leukaemia in its terminal stages; I'm afraid there is nothing we can do.'

Anne Belle watched as a solitary tear rolled down his cheek, just as it had that day in the ICU before he woke up. She watched his sadness, wondering at his reactions, realizing something more than the usual shock reaction was at work here. It was becoming clear that he loved her more than he had thought. This was a very serious affair.

She pulled up a chair and sat facing him. 'Sam,' she said gently, 'are you OK?'

'Anne, I can't lose her to this. I lost my mother to kidney failure. She only had one kidney. I offered one of my own but it wasn't possible. Now Cindy, my God, the first girl I have loved deeply in my life. Going the same way. Anne, can she have one of my kidneys?'

'It's too soon for this. She'll go on dialysis for however long it takes. We can tissue type you later. This is 2005, Sam. She'll be OK.'

He nodded. 'You're right, Anne. Sorry. Just brought it all back.'

She leaned over and hugged him. 'We'll get her through this, Sam, one way or another. I promise you. And when Anne Bell promises something, she delivers.'

He looked at her and managed an apology of a grin.

'So I've heard,' he said.

23

After grabbing the embryos, Simone was on another high. Peter was more restrained. 'Peter, what's wrong?' She asked, as they sat in the living-room drinking white wine.

'Nothing, Simone. I just don't feel good about this. That cop worries me. He wants to check on the Jeep. He's noticed the new bull bar and that the tyres have been changed.'

'So what? There's no proof to link us to any of this.'

'I just think we should shut up Copley, destroy the evidence, and get out of here. There's been enough damage done already.'

'What damage?'

'The biker. The girl. The kidnappings. Hell, Simone, if we're caught, it will be life, if not worse. It's time to quit. Let's go while we can.'

'Peter, just a little longer. We got the embryos. Let's start to wind Copley down, start to pack up here, get Lorene sorted, make as much as we can on the embryos and blow. Overnight. Let's give ourselves three weeks max then go. We could make a stack in that time, but we'll be ready to go at a moment's notice if that cop shows up again.'

'It's a risk, Simone. A big risk.'

She went over to him and kissed him full on the lips.

'Trust me, Peter. I've not let you down yet, have I?'

No, Peter thought. But the risks are getting worse by the day.

'OK, Simone. So long as we're ready to go stat. You always know best.'

★ ★ ★

Sam called Chris Hardy after work.

'Chris, it's Sam Brown. I need some help.'

There was a pause. She was not used to getting calls from senior surgeons at UHSM.

'Yes,' she responded slowly, 'like what?'

'I need Cindy's address.'

'Cindy, why?'

'Chris, I think you know I've been seeing a bit of Cindy since she left home. I know all about the beatings. Now she's in ICU at UHSM. She was raped and beaten last night. I think it was Billy. I need to find him.'

He heard the sharp intake of breath as Chris realized what had happened to her best friend. 'My God, Dr Brown, is she OK? Is it serious?'

'Very serious.' He told her the extent of Cindy's injuries.

'What can I do?'

'Same as me for now, leave it up to Anne Bell and the others. And pray. Chris, do you have that address?'

'It's 1395 Cedar Avenue, in the South Boston area. But, Dr Brown, shouldn't you be telling the police, leaving things up to them?'

'Chris, please call me Sam. I will, in time. For now I just want to make sure he hasn't left town. Wait till you see her. You'll want someone to reach the bastard before the police get there.'

'I'll go down there now, Sam. You track down Billy. But don't do anything stupid. I know you feel like beating his brains out, but think of yourself, think of Cindy when she gets through this. Just find him and call the police.'

It took Sam about twenty minutes to reach Cedar Avenue. He parked the car and walked up to the front door cautiously, looking around him the whole time. There was no answer to the bell. He wandered carefully round to the back yard but the place looked deserted. He wasn't sure what he was going to do if he had encountered Billy, but at least he knew now where he lived. He could call

239

again later. He returned to the car to drive back to the hospital trying to work out exactly what to do about Billy James.

★ ★ ★

That evening the party in the doctor's quarters was in full swing and Nick Bailey was having a good time. The music was deafening, the bar crowded, and the atmosphere magical. It was about 9.45 and Chris had promised to get there by 10.30 after her shift ended. Nick felt right at home behind the bar, dispensing beer and vodka and whiskey to anyone who asked. And they all approved of the Ozzie bartender who was doing such a great job — especially the brunette with the big equipment and the c'mon attitude.

As Nick interpreted it.

Orthopaedic nurse. He'd seen her before on a consult visit to the fracture ward and she'd given him a bit of come on then.

Confident girl, but you needed an attitude to survive in orthopaedics, he thought. All those young randy patients with broken limbs and frustrating splints, and all those aggressive surgeons with serious egos and attitudes.

What did they call that orthopod back in Melbourne who terrorized the department?

Dr Blockhead. He smiled at the thought. Gynaecologists got a bit of stick, but at least they weren't orthopods. Hammer and chisel merchants versus scalpel and forceps artists. So the nurses who looked after a Dr Blockhead had to be good. And aggressive. Know what they wanted. And there was no doubt what this one wanted.

It was only ten when she came up for her third refill.

'Thank you, Dr Bailey. The famous Dr Bailey. The Australian resident everyone loves and everyone wants to get to know better.'

She leaned over the bar and made to whisper in his ear. Instead of the whisper it was her tongue that gently entered his ear and made it very clear what was required of him.

He didn't pull away. He was quite enjoying it. He looked at her again. Not bad, he thought. Needing a quickie? That unexpected moment when two people, uncontrollably hot, find themselves together, in favourable circumstances, and just want to do it. Get on with it. Now! Quickly! Two minutes. No questions asked, no answers required. This opportunity may never happen again. Now or never. He'd been there, done it. It was almost part of growing up in med school. What was it his Manchester friends had called it? The

Accidental Fuck! So why not now?

'What's your name?' he asked.

'Sammy. Short for Samantha.'

'How's the drink?'

'Fine. That's not what I'm after, Nick. Why don't you and I just get out of here for a little while and find somewhere cosy to get to know each other?'

'You mean, really get to know each other?' he asked.

'Oh yes,' she said.

He felt a stirring in his nether regions and his old habits told him *why not?* He grinned and put down the bar towel making to move around to join her. He could see she was almost orgasmic with anticipation, seeing that he had gone for it. Then suddenly he stopped.

A vision of Chris leapt into his mind and brought him to a standstill. And he realized he couldn't go through with it. His mind was racing.

What's happening to you, Nick Bailey, he thought, turning down an open invitation like this? Hell, this is a first. You've never done anything like this before! What's going on?

But turn around he did with a mumbled, 'Sorry, Sammy, just can't make it tonight.' She stared at him in disbelief.

'Some other time, Nick,' she said, then turned and left, a disappointed look on her face. It was only a matter of minutes before his mobile went off.

'Nick? It's Chris. You OK?'

'Sure,' he said, 'only had a couple. Been working the bar. Where are you?'

'At the hospital. I know we were supposed to party tonight but Cindy James has been attacked. She's in ICU. She may not make it. So I'm going to stay with her.'

'Oh Chris, that's awful. I'll come over,' he said, suddenly grateful for the decision he had made a few moments before, and realizing that his life was changing by the minute.

'No, you don't have to leave the party — '

He interrupted her. 'I'll come over,' he said quietly.

★   ★   ★

The next morning, Sam Brown's secretary was waiting for him when he reached the office.

'Doctor Brown, Mrs McBride is waiting in your office. She turned up an hour or so ago without an appointment and insisted on seeing you.'

'It's OK, Rosemary, I'll see her,' he said, wondering what was in store for him now. Eleanor McBride stood up and turned to face him as he entered the office.

'Doctor Brown,' she said, walking towards him with her hand outstretched. Sam took the handshake and smiled.

'Eleanor, what can I do for you?'

They sat down on opposite sides of the large desk and Sam waited for her to respond.

'Bill and I had a long, serious talk last evening,' she said slowly. It was clear that this conversation was difficult for her. 'We decided that I should come clean with you after the lovely way you took care of me during my pregnancy. You asked for help and I refused. I overreacted. The truth is, Sam' — she took a deep breath before continuing — 'baby Patrick was not a natural conception. Bill is infertile. Patrick was the result of artificial insemination by a private gynaecologist.'

Sam almost groaned. The cluster theory was clearly about to be blown right out of the water. 'I see,' he said softly.

'Does it help to know?'

'Yes. Are you able to tell me who the gynaecologist is and where he practices?'

'Yes, but only if you tell me why you need to know.'

Sam swallowed. He needed to think fast. How could he tell this lovely proud mother that her son might be a clone of several offspring arranged by that same gynaecologist? Would it affect her relationship with her baby? Could it do irreparable harm to her? Or would it not affect her at all?

'Eleanor, we just don't know. As I told you before, there have been three cases of Holt-Oram syndrome in a very short time. We just have to follow them up, especially since one of the cases involves a homicide. Her mother was killed in a hit-and-run which the police have suspicions about.'

'I see. That is important,' She reached into her bag and pulled out a card. 'That is the name and address of the gynaecologist who treated me. I have to say that I hope very much that he is not involved. He gave me little Patrick and was very professional throughout. It cost a bundle but the result of his treatment is priceless. I think I would prefer not to know if he has done something terrible. It's just not relevant to me.' She stood up.

Sam walked around the table to join her. He put both his hands out and she took them.

'Eleanor, you are a wonderful woman. I know how happy you were with your pregnancy and birth. You will make a marvellous mother and I will always be here for you if I can ever help. What you have just done today took a lot of strength and courage. I will not abuse that in any way, at any time. I just want to say that if there has been wrongdoing, it must be stopped, and you will have helped enormously in that.'

'Thank you, Sam. Oh, I nearly forgot.' She reached into her bag again and brought out an envelope. 'I said no blood tests, but Bill said I should give you a couple of little Patrick's hairs. He said you can do DNA tests from them. You said you wanted to check up on the H-O gene.'

'Tell him thank you. You didn't have to pull out little Patrick's hair for me though!'

She smiled. 'It was quite painless. They were on his pillow!'

'Eleanor, I'm so pleased we are friends again.'

'Me, too, Sam. Bye.'

She left and Sam returned to his desk. He picked up the card and looked at it.

Dr Peter Mendova MD,
1171 Revere St,
Copley Square, Boston.

He didn't know the name, but he soon would. He would do a little research into this MD and then, if appropriate, he would call Joe Kennedy.

Joe Kennedy was leaving the precinct when his cell phone rang.

'Kennedy,' he barked, walking quickly down the corridor to the staff exit. He always walked quickly. You got more done that way.

'Joe, it's Anne Bell.'

'You're the only Anne I know, Anne; you don't have to be formal.'

There was silence for a few moments. He felt a small knot forming in his stomach. He could always sense danger. Always knew when bad news was on the way.

'What is it?' he asked quietly.

'Cindy James, the young nurse . . . '

'Who took care of Dr Brown, yes?'

'Yes. She's in my ICU, possibly dying. She was raped and beaten half to death two nights ago.'

'What? Who? Where? Did the precinct cops sort it? Have they caught anyone?'

'The local cops have been outside all along. They've not called you, Joe, because it's not homicide yet. But it might be. I haven't let them in — there's nothing they can do yet anyway. She was brought in on a 911 by paramedics after being found on the Common.'

'So there will be a team at the crime scene.

247

Do you know where it was exactly?'

'Not exactly. But that's not why I'm calling, Joe. I'm calling for a favour. I want you to get involved in this. It's personal now, very personal. Whoever did this is an animal. He made a real mess of Cindy. He has to be caught and I don't know anyone else I would trust to do it.'

'Oh I'll get involved all right, Dr Bell. It's not homicide, yet, but it's obviously damn close. I'll come in and speak to the local guys.'

'And then to me, Joe, there's more.'

'I'm on the way.'

Thirty minutes later he was standing beside Chris Hardy and Nick Bailey gazing down at Cindy James. He had seen similar cases many times over the years, but when it was someone you knew it was always worse. Anne watched him. Reading his thoughts, thinking it was just the same for medics. They could be completely objective for years until one of their family got sick. Then they reacted just like anyone else.

'You said there was more, Anne?'

'Come to the office.'

'Is she going to make it?'

'Maybe. Her only kidney is playing up. We can control that with haemofiltration — like dialysis,' she added, seeing his eyebrows raised at the unfamiliar word. 'It just means that she is more susceptible to other ICU complications, infection, respiratory trouble, things that can just add up to a point where all the organs simply fail.'

'I see. So what more is there?'

'Sam Brown feels more for this girl than we thought. I think he is very serious about her. His reaction to seeing her told me as much, and he more or less admitted it. Incidentally, he lost his mother to kidney failure — she only had one kidney also, so he's pretty low. But that's not it. When we first talked about it, he said it was her husband who did it. Straight out. No hesitation. Apparently there was a long history of domestic abuse. He saw her bruised several times recently. She had left her husband a few weeks ago after the worst beating.'

'I see. It seems possible. He's not been in to see her?'

'No, but he might not know if they are separated and he's innocent.'

'What does he do?'

'He's a cop, Joe. Well, an ex-cop.'

Joe's head lolled back and he stared at the ceiling. 'He would be,' he groaned. What's his name?'

'Billy, Billy James.'

'Do you have an address?'

'1395 Cedar Avenue.'

'OK, Anne. I'll get started. I'll keep you posted.'

She nodded and they left the office to look again at Cindy.

'Come on, Cindy,' Anne said to herself. 'You can do it.'

24

Sam Brown went from his clinic directly to the library. He sought out the Physician's Register and skipped the pages until he found Mendova. There were four Peters, two with New York addresses, two in the Midwest but none in Boston. It meant nothing. Some people forgot, or just didn't bother to keep their entries current. He decided to make a trip down to Copley and check it out for himself. He parked and took a walk down Revere Street pausing outside 1171. It was an impressive building serving several physicians whose plates were displayed on the front wall. Dr Peter Mendova occupied a suite on the second floor. He walked into the building and made for the office. Behind the glass-fronted door was a small reception area and waiting-room. There was no sign of the doctor. He paused for a moment then walked in. The receptionist looked up and smiled.

'Good afternoon, sir,' she beamed. 'Can I help you?'

'Yes, I was wondering if you had any brochures or information on the services on offer here?'

'Why yes,' she replied, reaching into her desk for the information. 'Is that what you wanted?'

Sam glanced at the handouts. On the back of one of them was the photograph of a young, handsome-looking man in a smart suit.

'Yes, that's fine, thank you.'

'I'm afraid the doctor isn't in at the moment. I'm expecting him at about 4 p.m.'

'That's OK, this will do for now.'

'Do you want an appointment to see him?'

'No, let me just check these out and I'll get back to you.'

He made for the door. Everything seemed completely normal about the practice. Did he have enough to speak to Joe Kennedy?

His cell phone rang as he made his way back to the car.

'Sam, it's Jules in pathology. Can you talk?'

'Sure. What have you got?'

'The DNA strands — they all have matching features. The hair you gave me, and the samples from Orphan Annie and the abandoned child. It's not conclusive, but it is more than highly suggestive that these children could be the progeny of one parent.'

Sam whistled softly. 'Thanks, Jules. Keep it to yourself for now, would you?'

'Sure. But tell me the whole story some day.'

'Will do.'

So, it *was* time to talk to the cop, he thought.

★ ★ ★

The cop in question was nosing around Cedar Avenue but the house seemed deserted. He rang the doorbell, keeping his finger on the button for thirty seconds before letting it go, then banged hard on the door, but there was no response. He peered through the windows, observing the mess of a badly neglected living-room. He decided to go back to the hospital and check on Cindy before going to the precinct to arrange a search warrant.

Sam Brown was at her side with Chris.

'How is she?' he asked, as he shook hands with Sam.

'Worse. Chest complications. ARDS. The lungs are packing up so she's not getting enough oxygen in spite of a hundred per cent on the ventilator. She's losing the fight, Detective.' His voice trembled slightly as he said the words.

'She's young and strong, Sam. She might pull through.'

Sam did not look convinced. 'Thanks, Joe. Now I've got news for you. Come with me.'

He led him away from the unit into the corridor telling him of his meeting with Eleanor McBride, and the results of the DNA tests.

'Holy cow, Doc, that's powerful evidence. And I know of this guy — he lives near where the hit-and-run occurred. I interviewed him at Copley. This makes him the top suspect.' Two search warrants, he thought. 'I need to go. Good luck with Cindy, Doc. Don't lose faith. We're all rooting for her, and Anne Bell's on the job.'

'Sure.'

Sam walked back into the ICU leaving Joe to go about his business. The ARDS was a new threat Cindy could do without. He was filled with a combination of desperation and rage, making him more than ever determined to call back to Cedar Avenue and seek out Mr Billy James.

He turned to Chris with a look of intense anger on his face. 'Keep an eye on her, Chris.'

'Are you going?'

'Yes, I'm going to finish my clinic, then I'm going to find that no-good bastard, Billy James, and teach him a lesson he's never going to forget.' •

'Oh, Sam, don't. You're so angry, you

254

might not be able to stop yourself. If . . . when . . . Cindy gets better she won't want you in a prison cell.'

'I won't kill him, Chris, but I will get him and bring him in. If there's a struggle . . . '

'Sam, he'll be desperate. Look what he did here. Be careful, he's a tough ex-cop.'

'I'll be careful. But I'm going for him, Chris, I'm going for him.'

And he turned and left, leaving Chris with her friend hanging on to the last thread of life.

★ ★ ★

Back at the precinct, Joe put the process of getting the search warrants in action. He asked for a double warrant for the Mendova case since he needed to look at the Copley consulting-rooms as well as White Plains. He wondered what sort of squad to assemble. He didn't want to take an army out there, but there was a probable murder on the record. In the end he picked just one young detective and one uniformed officer to accompany him. It was unlikely to be a violent exercise. The doctor and his wife simply needed to realize the game was up.

He dialled the Copley surgery to enquire if Dr Mendova was in and was informed that he was taking a day off.

Good, he thought. Then we'll do White Plains first.

★   ★   ★

Anne was in her office in the ICU when she heard Chris say 'Anne,' then louder, 'Doctor Bell.'

Anne got up from her desk and walked out, meeting Chris coming towards her.

'Come and look,' she said, turning to walk back to Cindy's bed.

'What is it?' she asked.

'Well, you know I'm a urological practitioner nurse?'

'Yes.'

'So I get interested in silly things, like whether anyone's peeing properly or not.'

Anne wasn't sure yet where Chris was coming from.

'Look at the bags.'

Underneath the bed were tubes leading to four bags. One tube from the inside of the damaged upper kidney, which had been draining urine steadily since insertion, one from the lower half of the same kidney doing the same, one from the area around the kidney which had drained for two days, then stopped. As they all wanted it to. And one

256

from the bladder, where all the urine should have been draining into. And into which not one drop had drained since Cindy had been admitted.

Until now.

'Look, Anne,' said Chris excitedly, pointing to the bags.

Of the four bags, three were empty. The bag from the catheter draining the bladder was a quarter full of clear, healthy-looking fluid.

'My God,' said Anne; then 'My God! Her kidney's working, and it's all coming the right way!' She turned to Chris who was beaming at her with excitement.

In spite of the fact that they were only discussing the elimination of waste body products, that is exactly the sort of thing that can make ICU doctors, and especially urological doctors and nurses very excited indeed. It was the first sign that Cindy might, after all, make it.

So Anne Bell and Chris Hardy did something doctors and nurses on an ICU don't do very often. They gave each other a big, noisy high five.

25

Joe Kennedy left for White Plains with Detective Steve Peters, and Dick Brown, the uniformed officer, followed in a squad car. When they reached the gates Joe got out. He looked at the intercom button. Then he decided to ignore it.

Better to turn up unannounced.

He walked round to the trunk and returned with the bolt cutter and lock buster. Within half a minute the gate was open and they entered the drive. He pushed the gate back behind them and ordered the uniformed officer to stay at the exit and prevent anyone leaving by any means. He and Peters then approached the house. Peters fingered the gun in his belt.

As they got out of the car and approached the front door, Joe spoke quietly, 'I'll go in alone and talk with them, Steve. You stay by the front door. At the first sound of any trouble, come in. Hopefully they'll come quietly.'

He rang the bell without a response. At the second ring he heard movement, steps heading towards them. Quiet, but natural, unhurried. The door opened to reveal a young woman with short blonde hair and blue eyes to match his own.

'Yes?' she said, with a clipped New York accent.

'Mrs Mendova?'

'No, Ms Belmont. Who wants to know?'

Joe pulled out his badge and flashed it at her. 'Detective Joe Kennedy, South Boston Police. Can I come in?'

She looked concerned suddenly, but she nodded and stepped back.

'He not coming?' she asked, indicating Steve Peters with a shake of her head.

'No, he'll watch things from out here. We'll leave the door open, please.'

She shrugged as if to say please yourself and led him through the hall to a large living-room on the right. Peter Mendova was standing in front of the mantelpiece, a glass of wine in his hand, the living gas fire making a warm centrepiece on a cold New England day. He saw Kennedy and a look of surprise passed over his face, in contrast to the almost carefree attitude of his companion.

'Ah, Detective, this is an unexpected visit,' he said putting the wine on the nearby table.

'Yes, Doctor, sorry about that. Can we sit?' He motioned to a four-seater settee and sat down at the opposite end to Peter Mendova.

Simone sat in a matching chair some distance away across the room.

'What is it?' asked Peter. 'What can we do for you?'

'I think you know we are investigating a hit-and-run accident near here some time ago. We spoke about your four by four, Doctor?'

'Yes. I remember.'

'Well, certain new evidence has come to light regarding your private practice which we believe needs clarification.'

'What sort of evidence? What the hell are you talking about, Detective?'

'The evidence, sir, relates to the possibility of illegal cloning as part of infertility treatment.'

'Cloning? What on earth do you mean?'

'I'll be happy to explain everything, but I have to ask that you both accompany me to the station so we can commence these enquiries on a formal basis.'

'Do you have an arrest warrant, Detective, because if not I will have to ask you to leave.'

'I think it would be more sensible if we could talk about this at the station.'

'I want to talk about it here,' said Simone, her voice icy and full of threat.

And confidence.

'That's not possible, ma'am. We can do it

the easy way, and you accompany us and co-operate, or we can do it the other way, and I enforce the search and arrest warrants in my pocket.'

Joe could see by now that Peter Mendova was sweating profusely, a look of pure horror on his face. He stared at Joe as if not believing what he was hearing, then back at Simone. In contrast, Simone was sitting straight and poised, staring at Joe with a look of pure venom, her eyes avoiding Peter's.

'I told you — ' Mendova started.

'Shut up, Peter,' she shouted, rising from the chair and pointing at Joe Kennedy.

Pointing a cocked .38 special.

Kennedy stood up. 'This won't help, ma'am.'

'Easy, Cop, easy . . . get your hands behind your head, *Now*!'

Joe slowly did so, wondering how he had got into this mess. Then wondering how he was going to get out of it.

'Get his gun, Pete.'

Peter looked at the cop and Simone in turn, like a confused rabbit in the headlamps of an oncoming car.

'Get his gun, Peter,' she said firmly.

He moved towards Kennedy cautiously, and took his gun from his belt.

'Right, Detective, we're moving down to

the cellar now, nice and easy.'

'You won't get away with this,' said Joe, wondering when or whether to call in Steve Peters. Would he hear him? Would she blow him away immediately he tried?

'Peter, bring the gun. We'll finish him off down there, then deal with the other one.'

'No.'

She paused. The voice was Peter Mendova's. Kennedy turned and his eyes widened.

Peter Mendova was pointing the cop's gun directly at Simone.

'Peter, what are you doing?'

'I said no, Simone. It's over. They've got us. Killing cops is not going to help.'

'Peter, bring the gun over here and do as I say.'

'No!' The voice was louder now, more insistent.

'One last time, Peter — '

'No Simone — it's over!'

The explosion shook the room and at first Joe Kennedy didn't know where it had come from. He just registered that he was still standing.

So was the girl.

Peter Mendova was slowly slipping to the ground, a smoking hole in his forehead spouting blood and brain.

Joe looked quickly at Simone but the pistol

had once more taken deadly aim at his own forehead. He saw her index finger whiten on the trigger and realized he had to make a move to get the gun out of Peter Mendova's dead hand.

Which was when Steve Peters burst in.

For one brief moment Simone shifted her aim to the newcomer and Joe knew he only had seconds as he went into a classic roll to the ground towards Mendova, whipping the gun from his hand, hoping against hope that Peter's entrance would cause Simone to falter.

He was wrong. Simone never faltered for a moment.

In the few seconds it took for Peters to come in and size up the situation before firing, and the few seconds it took for Joe Kennedy to reach the gun in Mendova's hand and fire also, Simone calmly put the gun to her own forehead and said quietly, 'You will never take us; you will never part us.'

A vision of herself and Peter in O'Reilly's Bar in New York on their first night together flitted through her brain.

The three explosions happened almost simultaneously, but Joe would always insist that Simone's shot was first.

The bullet went straight through her brain, exactly where she had shot Peter. Joe's bullet hit her in the throat, and Peters's bullet went right through her abdomen, and the tiny unborn baby she had never even told Peter she was carrying. She fell forward on to the ground, the gun clattering to the floor and her arm falling across the chest of her lover in a final bizarre embrace.

They moved carefully towards the prostrate body, but no care was needed. Joe felt for the carotid pulse as a matter of routine. There was none.

'We were lucky. You did good, Steve. Sorry to get you into this. Who could have predicted that this woman would be so tough?' He paused, shaking his head. Who *was* this woman who had been so determined and effective, prepared to kill cops and even her lover to get to freedom?

Then herself when she realized it was over.

He called the station. They wouldn't be coming in for questioning, he told them. They sent a meat wagon instead.

They turned to leave when they heard a sound upstairs. Joe looked at Steve, his index finger against his lips, and they drew their guns again.

Joe slowly led the way, stair by stair, his gun in his outstretched hands, trying to identify movement, breathing. He turned from the top stair into a broad landing. He stiffened suddenly, and the gun stopped moving and fell slowly to his side. Steve followed him, then gasped. Sitting on the landing floor, arms around each other, fear in their eyes, were two young girls.

'Who are you?' asked Joe.

'I'm Leanne, this is Lorene.'

'What are you doing here?'

There was silence for a moment, before Leanne said, quietly, 'I don't really know.'

* * *

Sam Brown was heading for the house at Cedar Avenue. *Les Mis* was roaring in his ears. The angry men were on the march and Sam was one of them.

He slowed down as he approached the house and switched the angry men down. There was a car parked outside so it looked like Billy was at home.

It was just turning to dusk but he could see no lights inside as he crept up to the back door. He took a deep breath then kicked it as hard as he could just above the lock. The door burst open and he ran inside.

He heard a noise in a bedroom above him.

'What the fuck . . . ?'

'That you, Billy James?' he called.

'Who wants to know?'

'Come on down, Billy, we need to talk.'

'Who is this? Get out of my house. I know the law. I've got a gun and I know how to use it. Just fuck off out of here.'

The voice was slurred and Sam knew he must have been drinking. Did that make him more or less dangerous?

'Come on, Billy. I just want to talk.'

'I'm not talking to anyone. Get out, or I'm coming down with this gun.'

'So come on, Billy. I'm not going anywhere.'

Sam was standing just inside the living-room at the bottom of the stairs. He had a fistful of coins to throw into the dining-room opposite to try to distract Billy when he came down. He had to get the gun. Equalize the odds. Then they could talk.

He heard the stair creak, then a stumble as if Billy had missed his step.

'Shit!' Billy James whispered, waving the gun from side to side, staring into the gloom. 'Where are you, creep? You're gonna die when I find you.'

He reached the bottom step and Sam launched the coins.

Billy followed the confusing sound and let off two shots just before Sam, with a kick to match any field goal kicker in the New England Patriots, kicked out at his gun and launched it harmlessly into the air. In the next moment he had a struggling Billy James

266

by the throat and launched a blow at his left eye. But, in spite of the drink, Billy James was not about to give up easily. His fists continued to flail out in all directions, which was when Sam hit him on the chin and Billy went down like a sack of potatoes.

★ ★ ★

Chris Hardy was worried. Less worried about Cindy now, but worried about Sam Brown as she remembered his behaviour earlier in the day. She left her friend's side and went to Anne Bell's office, knocking on the door before walking in.

'Doctor Bell, I'm a bit worried about Dr Brown.'

'Well, he's going through a lot — '

'No, I'm worried that he might do something stupid. He's gone off looking for Cindy's husband.'

'You mean, not *just* looking?'

'No. He's blind with grief and angry as hell.'

Anne rubbed her chin thoughtfully.

'Thanks, Chris. I'll call Detective Kennedy and let him know; see if he can head him off.'

Chris nodded and left. At the nurses' station she paused suddenly, then picked up the phone and put out an urgent page for Nick Bailey.

Head him off.

267

Joe was leaving White Plains when the cell phone rang again.

'What now?' he asked no one in particular, as he pressed the accept button.

'Joe?'

'Yes, Anne, is that you?'

'Yes. Chris has just told me that Sam is going after Billy James. Joe, he's angry. Very angry. Can you reach him before he does something stupid?'

'I'll try.'

'And, Joe, if you need to persuade him, tell him Cindy's just starting to show good signs. The ARDS is lessening, her kidney seems to be recovering. She might just make it. Tell him, Joe, and please ... please get there before it's too late.'

Sam looked over at Steve Peters. 'One more call before we go back to the precinct?'

'OK, Joe. Go for it.'

★ ★ ★

Chris drove faster than she had ever driven in her life while Nick gripped the front of the dashboard and prayed for their lives. Eventually they reached the house and leaped out. The front door was open and they dashed in not knowing what to expect, but determined to keep Sam Brown out of trouble.

★ ★ ★

It was only five minutes later when Joe Kennedy reached Cedar. 'Stay here, Steve. This one's my call.'

'I'll man the exit again, Joe. It worked last time.'

Joe reached for his gun and crept around the back of the house. He walked through the back door and then shouted out, 'Police, Anyone there?' As he walked further through the kitchen, he heard voices, then Chris's voice called out, 'Here, in the living-room.'

Joe followed the voice, his hand searching for the light switches. None of them worked. The power company must have cut Billy off.

He walked into the living-room and, in the gloom, saw the unmistakable figure of Sam Brown standing beside Chris Hardy and Nick Bailey, Sam looking angry, his right hand by his side, the fist opening and closing. Nick recalled the same movement in the OR that day when Sam lost the fight to save Shirley Brookes.

Fist opening and closing in anger and frustration.

Before them tied and slouched in a chair,

was the barely conscious figure of Billy James.

'Shit, Sam, have you killed him?'

'No, Joe. He resisted a citizen's arrest. I had to restrain him. But I tell you, if these two hadn't appeared, I might have done something very stupid.'

'He doesn't look too good.'

'He's more drunk than beaten up.'

'It's true, Detective,' said Nick. 'I've looked him over and he's OK, just very pissed and slightly concussed.'

'Glad to hear it, because the Anne Bell report says Cindy's showing signs of improvement. Be a shame if she spent her first day out of hospital visiting Dr Brown in prison. Even now, in theory, he's broken a few rules.'

'What do you want me to do?' asked Sam, with a resigned look on his face. 'You taking me in?'

'Get out of here all of you,' said Joe. 'Go to Cindy. Let me take it from here. I'll catch you later.'

Nick and Chris exchanged relieved glances, thanking their lucky stars they had decided to come to Cedar Avenue. It had been one furious Sam Brown they had encountered there and it had taken a lot of persuasion to make him see sense.

'OK, thanks, Joe. I appreciate it.'

'Thank you. You apprehended him. Just

don't tell anyone. And thank these two for possibly saving your bacon.'

As they left, Joe Kennedy went to the kitchen and filled a jug with water. He returned to the living-room and threw the contents of the jug in Billy James's face.

Billy shook his head as consciousness returned. 'What's going on?' he asked, in his usual slurred voice.

'You resisted arrest. I am Detective Joe Kennedy from South Boston. I have here a search and arrest warrant with your name. You can remain silent. Anything you say may be used against you.

'Where's the big black guy?'

Joe looked around the room. 'Big black guy? I don't see anyone else here.'

'There was a big black guy. He assaulted me, tied me up.'

'Listen, you miserable apology for a human being, you are drunk out of your mind. You're imagining things here.'

He quietly cut the thin rope binding Billy to the chair as he spoke, and it fell to the floor without Billy even noticing.

'I am Detective Joe Kennedy. You are being arrested for the rape and attempted murder of Nurse Cindy James, your wife. I am convinced that DNA tests will prove you were the perp. I've come here to arrest you and

271

bring you in. You resisted arrest. I had to restrain you. Got it?'

Billy James looked confused. Joe pulled him roughly to his feet, gripping his arm so tight Billy winced with pain.

'And listen. You're an ex-cop. You disgust me. If you make even a try at resisting arrest again, or talk more rubbish about big black guys, I'll beat the fucking shit out of you. Or worse.' So saying he took his gun out of his belt, and pushed the barrel firmly into Billy's left nostril. 'Do you understand?'

Billy nodded.

Joe knew he had got the message.

He dragged him out to the yard where Steve Peters cuffed him, pushed him into the back of the car and got in beside him. Joe got into the driver's seat and they made for the precinct. He was exhausted, but all in all, it had been a pretty good day's work.

26

Three days later, Sam Brown was sitting at Cindy's bedside in the high dependency unit. She had been taken off the ventilator the day before, and was progressing well — fully conscious, taking oral fluids. He was holding her hand.

'They tell me the nephrostomy tubes will be out tomorrow,' he said. 'You could be home in a week or so.'

She smiled at him. 'Home?' she asked. She had no home anymore.

'My place. I want to take care of you. When you're better, you can decide whether it becomes your new home or not, but I want you to stay. If that's pushing things too fast, I'll help you find a place of your own.'

'We'll see, Sam. I don't want to put on you. Chris will probably insist that I stay with her. Either way, I'm not going anywhere. And I do want to be with you, you know that.' She squeezed his hand, then shut her eyes. Within a few seconds she was sleeping.

He got up quietly so as not to wake her, and walked out of the HDU up the corridor to Anne Bell's office.

She was sitting with Joe Kennedy.

'Hello again,' said Joe, standing up and shaking his hand.

The day before, Sam had accompanied Joe to Copley where they had found the records and equipment of Peter Mendova's gynaecology practice. Sam could hardly believe how they had run their illicit service with so little professional equipment. He still felt anger at the way they had abused the system, and misled particularly vulnerable patients with their greed and desire to get rich quick.

'Joe was just telling me about Mendova and your trip to Copley,' said Anne. 'He was a doctor, but not the specialist he claimed to be?'

'Exactly,' Sam said, 'and they restricted their practice entirely to infertility and artificial insemination.'

'And kidnapping illegal surrogates,' said Joe, 'drugging them, getting them pregnant to sell the babies. Street junkies I think. One of them is a sweet girl called Leanne. As she came down from the drugs and hypnotism, she began to recall details. She's got a lot to tell us still.'

'My God,' said Anne quietly.

'And let's not forget the murder of what was surely another pregnant surrogate escaping their clutches, and the poor biker who stopped to help her,' he added.

'Which one of them did that, Joe?'

'No proof. But it had to be her. My impression is that she was the brains, the dominant one. She pulled the gun; she decided to finish me off in the cellar. He just did what he was told. Until unexpectedly he saved my life.'

Anne broke the ensuing silence. 'Anyway, the good news is Cindy is well on the road to recovery.'

'Thanks to you, Anne,' said Sam. 'You did the double, first me and now Cindy. What can I say?'

'Just be happy, Sam. Be happy together. You've both earned it.' She squeezed his hand and turned to Joe.

'So, what for you now, Detective Joe Kennedy?'

He leaned back in the chair, grinning his lop-sided grin. 'Well, until you guys come up with yet more medical mayhem to fill my hours, I've got two choices. I've got a mountainous, overflowing in-tray back at the office, and I've got two tickets to Disneyworld back home. After what I've seen in the last few months, I think a little Mickey, Tinkerbell and the Magic Kingdom might just redress the balance.'

'So screw the in-tray?' asked Anne, innocently.

'Again,' he replied, and got up to leave.

He shook Sam's hand warmly and Anne followed him out of the ICU to the elevator. As they waited, she turned to him and said, slowly and quietly, 'Joe Kennedy, you are a hell of a guy.'

He put his arms around her gently and they hugged each other, the tough cop and the tough Director of ICU, hugging warmly and affectionately, not separating until the elevator door opened. He stepped inside, and turned to face her.

'And you, Dr Anne Bell, are a hell of a girl.'

The doors closed slowly. She stood there for a moment, staring at them, realizing how much she liked and respected this cop, and wondering why all the best men she ever met were already accounted for.

Then, with a long sigh, she turned and walked back slowly to the Intensive Care Unit.

Remembering the hug.

We do hope that you have enjoyed reading this large print book.

Did you know that all of our titles are available for purchase?

We publish a wide range of high quality large print books including:
Romances, Mysteries, Classics
General Fiction
Non Fiction and Westerns

Special interest titles available in large print are:
The Little Oxford Dictionary
Music Book
Song Book
Hymn Book
Service Book

Also available from us courtesy of Oxford University Press:
Young Readers' Dictionary
(large print edition)
Young Readers' Thesaurus
(large print edition)

For further information or a free brochure, please contact us at:
Ulverscroft Large Print Books Ltd.,
The Green, Bradgate Road, Anstey,
Leicester, LE7 7FU, England.
Tel: (00 44) **0116 236 4325**
Fax: (00 44) **0116 234 0205**

SEEDS OF DESTRUCTION

A.V. Denham

When Joe set up separate homes with Amanda and Sara he sowed the seeds of destruction. Living with each of them for half the week, he used his deceased Aunt Ethel as an alibi for spending so much time away from his families . . . But the domestic calm becomes threatened, especially when Amanda's son, Simon, meets Harriet, the daughter of Sara . . . As the two women discover Joe's deception, they must sort out their lives. Would it all prove too much for Joe? Could living as one family solve their problems? Can there ever be an acceptable resolution?

SILENT SHADOWS

Eva Maria Knabenbauer

The Berlin Wall has fallen and Anni visits Aschersleben, the East German town she escaped from when she was twenty. The visit awakens memories of oppression and a passionate love affair. Victor, Anni's friend, accompanies her, and their relationship deepens. But she resists commitment as she tries to come to terms with her past. When Anni finds Karin, her school-friend, it's a painful experience, revealing a number of bitter truths. A new, invisible wall is bringing disharmony in an atmosphere where old grievances die slowly as justice is sought.

FLOWERS FOR THE JOURNEY

Louise Pakeman

Thirty, Clare reflects on her birthday, is a milestone in her life. Despite being a successful lawyer with a comfortable lifestyle in Melbourne, she feels that she's in a rut, particularly in her relationship with Robert. She wonders whether she wants to remain in it forever. And then a surprising letter amongst her birthday cards prompts Clare to take a holiday to meet the person who penned it, and a man and a dog with the power to change her life. With the security she has earned, dare she choose this alternative future?

THE MORNING PROMISE

Margaret James

Rose Courtenay's wealthy parents expect her to marry a neighbour's son and then settle down in Dorset. But the outbreak of the Great War offers Rose an unlikely opportunity to escape . . . Longing for adventure, she trains to be a nurse and is sent to France where the stark reality of war forces her to grow up fast. And then she falls in love with a man she can never marry. As the war ends, Rose must make the most difficult choice between her family, wealth and comfort, and the man she loves.

THE WIFE

Meg Wolitzer

Joe and Joan Castleman are en route to Helsinki. Joe is thinking about the prestigious literary prize he will receive and Joan is plotting how to leave him. For too long Joan has played the role of supportive wife, turning a blind eye to his misdemeanours, subjugating her own talents and quietly being the keystone of his success . . . This is an acerbic and astonishing take on a marriage and the truth that behind the compromises, dedication and promise inherent in marriage there so often lies a secret . . .